It was the third day of the war when I returned from tour: major European cities, Paris, Berlin, Brussels, London.

I was whacked.

The tour had been a great success; and all that went with it had been fast and furious. Newspapers, TV stations, receptions, smile, smile, smile. I was really truly whacked.

My jaw hurt from smiling.

My eyes were worn out with sparkling.

I don't mean to be a begrudger, but when something is over it is over and you should legitimately be able to relax.

At the party in London on the last night of the tour, the second day of the war, I had kissed Max Fischer, one of our producers, and said, 'You can count me out for New York. I ain't going to Noo York.' I scooted away from his reaction, which after a pause had been a hearty, angry laugh.

It had only been a rumour that had run around the company, but I knew that he had high hopes of Emmys and

Oscars or whatever they're called, best thises and thats, dinners at Sardi's and fat men thumping him on the back and handing him cigars ... maybe of course I've seen too many movies about show business. Thirty-seven weeks of *The Playboy* was enough for me, probably for ever. I had decided when the curtain came down that final night that next time round I would play the Widow Quinn and leave Pegeen to someone younger.

I know I've said it before but I really was whacked.

All I wanted to do was get back to my house in Goatstown, to Charlie, and pig out in front of the TV eating chocolates and watching the war.

I love chocolates.

I love Charlie too.

Yes.

And my house. I had bought it ten years earlier after I had made my first film and when it was still possible to buy a house before you'd made your first million. Now the amount I had paid would scarcely get you a tool shed in someone's backyard. The house has a back garden about fifteen yards long. A few neat rows of vegetables at the far end, away from the house; a patch of grass, two plum trees and some quite well-tended flower beds at each side. There is a stone terrace between the house and the grass and here I grow herbs in tubs: parsley, thyme, sage, chives, basil (when the weather is very warm), mint, chervil and feathery flags of fennel.

I suppose you could call me a landed person.

Queen of all I survey as long as I look due west and blinker my eyes, like a nervous racehorse, with my hands. If I disposed of the vegetables I could fit a croquet lawn between the terrace and the fence at the far end. This is a serious cause for consideration.

Goatstown was by no means my first choice; I would have preferred a neat little house by the sea, Sandycove, Dalkey, that way, but the money wouldn't run to it. Now, though I probably have the money, I am happy here, with my house, with my neighbours. By and large we are a friendly bunch in this street; we smile at each other, pass the time of day, we take in parcels if needed and keep spare keys for moments of crisis.

Don and Jenny live on my right with their four children. A few weeks ago, while I was away, their father put up a mini-goal for them halfway down the grass and now they spend their evenings smashing goals home and swearing at each other. I think they enjoy the swearing as much as the scoring of goals.

I envy those children. I was never allowed to swear and I had no one with whom to play football when I was twelve, twenty-three years ago. Of course in those days football did not have the status that it does now. Even small babies being pushed in their buggies are dressed in the raucous colours of their parents' favourite team. No pink for a girl and blue for a boy any longer; they are colours too insipid for the modern infant.

My neighbours on the other side have no children; they have instead sleek cats, who sit on our party wall flicking their tails, or lie quite motionless under one of my plum trees waiting for some unsuspecting bird to hop by. I have always envied the cat its capacity for being quite motionless.

I was whacked.

Bloody, deadly whacked.

I was sitting, feet up, on the sofa, watching the war on the television. Outside the spring was definitely starting; the evening sun was sliding down behind the hill, dappling the tops of the plum trees and flashing in the upstairs windows. On the screen words fell from the mouths of purposeful men. An American officer had just said with authority: 'They're not pausing. They are simply regrouping and considering their next move.' Light flashed behind him as he spoke; a huge golden ball spiralled in the sky. He looked very clean and well fed. Two small children appeared with their hands in the air, their black eyes rigid with fear. I heard the sound of the key in the door, then a pause and then the door slammed. 'Now over to Rageh Omaar in Baghdad . . .'

He threw his briefcase onto the hall floor and slung his coat over the end of the stairs.

I heard his step behind me.

'Isn't he sweet?' I asked.

'This is Charlie.'

'You're sweet too.'

He touched my hair with a casual hand. At the time I didn't know it to be casual.

'War games', he said.

'Unhunh.'

'Who's winning?'

'Who do you think?'

'No one.'

'Top of the class.'

I switched off beautiful Rageh Omaar.

We always eat in the kitchen unless we have visitors.

The room is a cheerful bright yellow, with doors that open onto the terrace, where, in the summer, my herbs scent the air. I am quite proud of that.

About eight thirty that evening the sun had gone, but the children next door were still shooting goals before they went to bed.

Move, you fucking asshole. Get your bloody feet off the ground. Now. Now, motherfucker. Oooo Jesus Christ, why can bloody girls not kick? I quit. The sound of a ball crashing into a flower bed. A door slams. Distant tears. Muuuummy.

Charlie stood by the window rubbing at a glass with a drying-up cloth. Squeak.

'Where would you like to have coffee?'

Squeak.

'Here or in the other room?'

Squeak.

I put two mugs on a tray and watched the steam coming from the spout of the kettle. From next door came the sound of raised voices. Normal bedtime war games.

'Don't do that. It makes me feel sick.'

I poured water over the ground coffee.

'Charlie.'

He put the glass down and dropped the cloth on the floor.

'Here. This is OK. Here. Sit down. There's something I . . . something I . . .'

I put the coffee pot on the tray beside the mugs and sat down.

'. . . have to say.'

His forehead wrinkled. He came across the room and sat down.

There was a long silence.

I pushed down the plunger in the coffee pot. 'Cat got your tongue?'

He smiled briefly. 'I'm not quite sure how to put this.'
Another silence.

I poured out two mugs of coffee and shoved one across
the table towards him. 'You're leaving me,' I suggested
facetiously.

The steam from the cups drifted between us.

'Joke,' I said.

'Yes, I mean, no. It's not a joke. I'm leaving you.'

'Charlie . . .'

He held up a hand, like policemen used to do all those
years ago, on point duty. The flat side of his hand was
towards me; I studied the lines patterning the palm: life
lines, health lines, personality lines, success and failure lines.
Nowhere could I see a this-is-the-end-of-a-marriage line.
Nowhere. I leant closer. He was saying something to me.
My heart was growing inside my chest. I could feel it filling
the cavity in there; I could feel the thunder and beat of it
growing. I wondered what would happen when the space
was full. Would pain start? I hated pain. Would . . .

He was tapping with a finger on the table.

'You're not listening to me, Sally. You have to listen to me.'

I grabbed my mug and swallowed a mouthful of boiling
coffee. That was pain. I choked.

'Sorry. I'm sorry. Could you say it all again. I'm listening
now.'

'I – am – leaving – you.'

He spoke each word separately, quite clearly.

'Yes. I heard that. But I don't understand. Is this some foreign language that you're speaking? I need some translation.'

'For God's sake, Sally, don't try and be clever. I hate it when you do that. Four words. English words. I am leaving you.'

There was a very long silence while I tried to force the words into my brain.

'Going,' he said at last. 'Clearing out.'

Tappity tap tap went his finger on the table.

'I think we need to talk about this. I think . . .'

'There's not much to say.'

'There has to be. Years of saying. Why? You have to tell me why. Honestly, Charlie . . . I thought we were good together. I thought we were happy.'

'It isn't working.'

'We seem to be happy. Aren't we as happy as everyone else?'

He shook his head. 'Maybe you're happy. Maybe you don't know what happiness is.'

'Oh Charlie.'

I felt tears building up behind my eyes. I blinked ferociously to make them stay there. He hated tears, I knew that.

'Charlie . . .'

His finger tapped viciously.

I took a deep breath.

'If this isn't working, can't we try and make it work? Tell me what I can do. Please. What have I been doing wrong?'

'You haven't been doing anything wrong. It just isn't working any longer. You know ... you know ... you know.'

'I don't know. Please tell me. I'm sure we can ... we don't need to do anything drastic. Is it ... is it babies? Charlie.'

'No. It's not babies. We've been through all that. Time and again. I feel, oh God this sounds so stupid, oppressed. Yes. That's it. Oppressed is the right word. I walk in here each evening and I feel oppressed, imprisoned. My life, this life, has become a prison.' He seemed quite pleased with that explanation. 'Yes. That's it.'

He stopped tapping with his finger and got up and walked over to the garden door and looked out. There was a streak of orange where the sun had been.

'But Charlie ... I haven't been here for ages, weeks and weeks. How can you feel imprisoned? Hunh? How can you possibly feel oppressed?'

He frowned. He stepped a little one, two, three with his feet. He rattled the coins and keys in his trousers' pocket.

'You always fidget,' I said.

'Excuse me?'

'It doesn't matter.'

I wondered how I had allowed this to happen.

I filled my coffee cup again.

How had I so misunderstood the nature of marriage? I truly believed that what we had was liberty. Love, friendship, liberty. Now he talks oppression. Now. This moment, here in our kitchen.

Unasked-for tears were rolling down my cheeks. I wiped them away with my fingers.

War games.

The image of those two Iraqi children with their hands in the air.

'So.'

The word came at me across the room like a hand grenade. It startled me.

'What does "so" mean?'

'What do you have to say? You have retreated into silence. You have to say something.'

I considered for a moment.

'There's not much I can say, is there? You seem to have this all thought out. I have been taken by surprise. I was in no way prepared for this. You have your mind made up. A fait accompli. "So" is not helpful. No. I presume you want me to pat you on the head and say run along darling, I'm sorry this hasn't worked out. I hope you enjoy the rest of your life.'

He stood there quite still, a slightly amused smile on his face.

'Fuck you. How's that for something to say?'

'Thanks.'

I picked up my mug of coffee and threw it at him.

It was a palpable hit: one grey suit temporarily ruined; one white shirt streaked with brown; one tie a goner; one face startled and then reproachful. Put your hands in the air, bastard.

'Sally . . .' he said. I leant across the table and picked up his mug and hurled it at him also. He was rooted to the ground. I got him on the shoulder.

More sartorial damage.

I put my head on the table and began to cry.

'This is a totally ridiculous way to behave,' he yelled at me. 'Have you lost your mind? This is my new suit.'

As if I cared.

'Look at it. Just bloody look at it.'

He took off the jacket and waved it round. Drops scattered everywhere. I wondered if the Figgises next door could hear him shouting through the wall. It would, I thought, be a nice change for them.

'And my shirt.'

He tore off his tie and flung it on the ground. Seventy pounds. Italian silk. Fit for nothing.

'Bastard,' I yelled at him.

'I am going up to change and when I come down, I hope you will have collected your wits.'

I looked over at him standing there by the glass door with his dripping coat in his hand. How absurd we are, I thought. I wiped my face with my fingers and then scrabbled in my pockets for some Kleenex.

'And while you're up there, pack.'

'Pack?'

I blew my nose. 'If you're leaving, you have to pack.'

'I wasn't intending to leave tonight.'

'And please take your dirty washing with you.'

'I wasn't . . .'

'When then? When were you intending . . .?'

'Well . . . in a few days . . . I have to . . .'

'Tonight.'

I waved my hand towards the door. 'Go and pack.'

'I can't possibly . . .'

I looked ostentatiously at my watch. 'You have all night. It is almost nine now. You usually leave for work at eight thirty. That gives you . . .'

'Sally. Be reasonable.'

'Sorry, what was that word you used?'

'Oh for Christ's sake, I hate it when you behave like this. Come on, let's sit down and talk this through.'

I left the room. I couldn't bear looking at him another moment. His silk vest was stained with coffee also. Even in the summer he wore silk vests; his mother, he had told me, had cajoled him into the habit while he was still at school. 'They help you to keep an even body temperature,' she had told him. 'Like a second skin.' Pah! I got the dustpan and brush and a little blue cloth and went back into the kitchen. He was still standing in the same place.

'Still here?' I asked. 'Wasting good packing time.'

I knelt down and began to pick up the pieces of the mugs scattered on the floor.

' "Yellow and black and pale and hectic red, pestilence-stricken multitudes," ' I muttered as I swept the shards into the pan.

'Look, Sally, tomorrow . . .' His voice was conciliating.

'Tonight. Unless of course you are merely winding me up. Hunh?'

'No, I'm not.'

'Then tonight. You want to leave. You leave. Take all your stuff with you when you go. I will be changing the locks tomorrow, so don't feel you can keep coming back whenever you feel like it. This is my house, Charlie, and I don't want you in it any longer.'

'There are things to discuss.'

'Not much.'

I was rubbing at the coffee on the floor with the blue cloth. He moved towards the door, stepping warily round me as though he thought I might attack him if he took his eye off me. As he reached the door he stopped.

'I'll arrange things tomorrow. I'll move out tomorrow. After all where can I go at this time of night.'

'Mummy.'

'Sally . . .'

'Or . . .'

I let the word hang on the air between us. An acrobat of a word on a high wire. He frowned and looked down at his shoes, pale beige slip-ons, splattered with coffee.

'I don't know what you mean by that.'

'I mean I'm not as green as I'm cabbage-looking.'

I rubbed at the floor.

'There are cardboard boxes in the garage, if you need them.'

He turned without a word and left the room.

I sat back on my heels and listened as he ran up the stairs and along the passage. The loo door slammed and I heard the lock click. After a moment or two he flushed water and the pipes rattled; the pipes always rattled when you flushed the loo, no plumber had ever been able to sort that out. I

heard the quiet urgency of his voice speaking on his mobile.
I got up from the floor and went over and switched on the
radio. Solemn voices were discussing the war. It seemed to
me that someone had always been discussing a war, the
possibility of a war, the ending of a war, the aftermath of a
war. I twiddled the knob; voices, music scuttled past my
ears, static jumbled sound scraped at the inside of my head.
Then someone playing a lonely saxophone, with a little riff
of a drum in the background. That was me all right. Yeah.

Outside the orange had faded from the sky and upstairs
Charlie, having finished talking to her, was opening drawers,
throwing cases from the top of the press down onto the
bed, his pale slip-ons shuffling on the floor as he moved.
No doubt he was feeling sorry for himself.

Hard done by.

No doubt at all.

End of a marriage.

An era.

I've lost the only playboy of the western world.

Bugger you Pegeen Mike.

The sax held a long sobbing note.

A child next door cried.

I sat down on the sofa and let my head fall back into the
cushions.

I must have sat there for about an hour, my mind quite

blank and dark. The jazz had long faded and someone was singing 'Un Bel Di' when Charlie came into the room. I struggled to focus my mind. The only thing I could think was, thank God nobody's talking about war.

'Un Bel Di' is better than that . . . not much, mind you.

Charlie walked across the room and switched off the radio.

'That's the most of it,' he said.

He unplugged the radio and stood with it in his hand looking down at me. 'I'll be back tomorrow for the bits and pieces.'

'You won't get in tomorrow.'

'There's my sound system and all my CDs to pack up. I'll take this with me now.' He waggled the radio at me.

'That's mine,' I said.

'Absolutely not.'

'That is mine, you big fart. You gave it to me for my birthday.'

He thought about that.

'Thirty,' I said. 'But take it if you want. The world won't come to an end. Just don't lie about it. If you've finished upstairs, I'm going to bed.' I got myself up from the couch. 'I mean what I said about tomorrow. You have all night to get your stuff out of here. All of it. Don't forget your silver christening mug and all your school photographs.'

'Sally . . .'

'I'll be here all day until the locks are changed. Goodnight, snake in the grass.' I climbed over the boxes and case in the hall and went upstairs.

I lay on the bed, fully clothed, and listened to the sounds below of my life being broken apart.

I have never been lucky with men.

This may possibly have to do with the fact that I have no father.

I have never had a father.

Nor brother, nor cousins; no male figure in my life to either love or hate.

So maybe my perceptions of how a male–female relationship should be are all wrong.

I have a grandfather.

He doesn't have any time for me. To give him his due he remembers Christmas and birthdays; a neatly folded cheque arrives in the post. No words on a card. No signs of affection. Nothing ever came from my grandmother, but he at least acknowledged my existence on such important days. Sometimes my mother had to bring me to his house, but she would make me sit outside in the car while she was inside, arguing with him. At least I presume she was arguing. Her lips were thin and taut when she came out, there was a touch of red round her eyes and she seldom spoke in the car on the way home.

I learnt quite quickly not to ask questions.

My mother was mother and father to me; and I suppose you might say grandmother and grandfather, brother and sister . . . When, of course, she wasn't too preoccupied in making ends meet.

'I have to make ends meet,' she would say. 'You have to help me make ends meet. Remember, Sally, the main thing you must learn is the importance of making ends meet.'

The major effect this has had on me is that I am now a slave to extravagance. I buy clothes I never wear. I have wonderful soft leather handbags, jumbo-sized bottles of Mitsouko, all sorts of gadgets that break. I have furs and furbelows, I buy first-class tickets on long-haul flights, I love champagne and I have almost as many shoes as Imelda Marcos.

And, of course, this house.

My house.

My bargain house.

When I told my mother about the house she had clicked her tongue against her teeth. 'Tuttt.'

'It was a bargain, Moth.'

I had called her Moth ever since I had begun to notice the vagaries of English spelling.

'You should be pleased with me instead of complaining. Wait and see. You'll be proud of me one day. I'm really going to be something. I'm never going to need to make ends meet.'

She hadn't been able to wait long enough.

She hadn't waited around to see my little red-lipped Norah in *The Plough*, Pegeen Mike or, my favourite so far, Sonya in *Uncle Vanya*. That I played at the National. She would have loved that. She might even have come all the way to London to see me.

Poor Moth.

We had never really seen eye to eye.

When I was a child she had wanted me beside her all the time; at her elbow or, like an obedient dog, at her heel. I never had friends round to play as the other children did, and I was seldom given permission to go to other girls' houses.

I turned in on myself . . . those were the words of Mrs Murdoch who came once a week to do the scrubbing; she was a buxom woman with no teeth. She never ate her crusts; she left them ranged on the side of her plate in a little wall. This did not go unnoticed by me.

'Mrs Murdoch never eats her crusts.'

'Mrs Murdoch has no teeth, for heaven's sake.' Then after a moment's thought Moth realised that she held all the cards. 'She has no teeth because she didn't eat her crusts when she was a child. Her mother never made her.'

'I don't like crusts.'

'Just eat them.'

Such shallow memories clutter my brain.

'That child will turn in on herself without pals. Kiddies need pals. Even if you've half a dozen of them like I did, they need pals from outside. I'm telling ya.'

I always listened to other people's conversations.

I had no alternative.

'The world,' she went on. 'You have to let her get used to the world. The earlier the better I say.' She waved her gnarled hands in the air for a moment and then left the room, heavy-footed.

Two of her children had died of consumption. It took me several years to discover that this did not mean they had eaten too much.

'Consumption has been eradicated in this country now,' I heard Moth say to Mrs Murdoch one day.

'Not soon enough for me.' Her voice was angry as she spoke the words. 'Not near soon enough.'

'Thanks to Dr Noel Browne,' said Moth.

'Godless communist,' replied Mrs Murdoch, with venom.

'I don't really think so, Mrs M.'

'Didn't he speak back to the Archbishop? He did. Didn't he try to pull us down into the mire of communism? He did. Oh yes, he did that.'

Moth sighed.

I never could work out why she started such conversations with Mrs Murdoch; she was always the flustered loser.

I relish such fragments.

I learnt to disappear when adults talked to one another, become invisible, not in any way stir the air around me.

I learnt their lines and intonations. I noticed their tremors, their stillnesses. I recognised as a child that by and large people were less happy than they pretended.

When I started to become an actress all those years of watching and listening served me in good stead. I found a use for my observations of other people's habits. I can pull gestures, tones of voice, facial expressions from the rag-and-bone shop of my heart like a conjuror pulls a rabbit from a hat.

Easy-peasy as the children next door shout . . . no. No, I am wrong: nowadays they shout, 'Fucking easy-peasy.'

Moth would hate that if she were still around to hear it.

She also would have hated the notion that I was watching, absorbing things in the way I did. Searching for secrets, instead of getting on with the job of growing up able to make ends meet. I think that was her only dream, that Sally should be able to make ends meet.

I probably malign her. She must at some stage have had hopes and aspirations, but by the time I came into her life she lived under the shadow of a depression that came and went without warning. One moment she might be playing some cheerful game with me in the park and the next her face would change, her hands tense and she would withdraw into silence and anxiety for maybe weeks at a time. She would go through the motions of normality, cooking meals, washing clothes, collecting me from school. There was no one in the shell of her body.

And then five years ago there was not even the shell any more.

On the table by her bed she had left instructions about cremation.

The note was short and to the point:

I can't go on. Please forgive me. I would prefer to be cremated. I do not want either God or my father at my funeral.

The note was written in her small neat writing and lay beside the empty bottle of pills and a jug of water. The glass had fallen from her hand at some moment and lay on the floor in glittering shards.

I suppose those few words were all that were needed.

Personally, I would have liked some expression of love or even an acknowledgment of my existence. 'Goodbye Sally' might even have done.

She wasn't old. She wasn't ill; she just couldn't bear living any longer.

It must have taken an energy that I didn't know she had to shovel all those pills into her mouth and wash them down with glass after glass of water.

I stared at her. She looked as if she had been manufactured from tissue paper, folded and smoothed, quite insubstantial.

'Dear Moth,' I heard myself say and then I realised that I was crying. 'Poor, poor Moth.'

The Ban garda standing beside me touched my arm. 'Can I get you . . .'

'Poor Moth.'

'. . . a cup of tea? A glass of water?'

I shook my head, 'Poor Moth.'

Poor. Poor. Poor.

I heard the sound echoing round her bedroom.

Poor.

Poor.

Poor.

There was a little cough.

Poor . . .

Tears flooded down my cheeks.

A touch on the arm.

A handkerchief held out in front of me.

'Thank you,' I said. I took it and wiped my eyes and face.
With a great effort I looked towards the body on the bed.
'Yes,' I said. 'That's my mother all right.'

She nodded.

I folded up the handkerchief and put it in my pocket.

'You must lose a lot of handkerchiefs.'

She smiled. 'A fair number. Will I leave you with her for
a while?'

'Oh no. No, please don't.'

That was all really.

I didn't cry again that day. There woke in me at that
moment, as I stood there by her bed, a very strong need to
find my father.

No. It wasn't like that.

No, no. No.

Nothing strong. Just a weak and fretful feeling. A seeping
through my veins.

Who is my father?

Where in the whole world is he?

Alive or dead?

Why is he not here?

For me.

Down the years I had asked my mother those questions
and others.

'Moth, why do I not have a father?'

'Because you don't.'

'I must have a father. Everyone has a father. I've learnt that much in school.'

She sighed.

'You have no father, Sally. How many times do I have to tell you?'

Over and over I had asked such questions and she had lied to me.

I of course had been aware that she was lying to me.

I gave up asking questions and let the thought of my father simmer in my head. There was nothing else to do.

*　*　*

I was awakened by the telephone ringing.

With difficulty I pulled open my eyes.

I had slept, but had dreamt non-stop of war: crying children, lost children, mutilated children. Women in black like huge crows flying in the air, mad with grief. It was a dream out of which I could not fight my way, so the sound of the telephone was like a lifeline to me.

The sky outside the window was a shining blue, no crows, no screams. I felt happy to be awake, but after a moment remembered. His side of the bed was empty. The telephone was ringing. I put out my hand and picked it up.

'Hello.'

'Hey there. Are you still asleep?'

It was my agent.

I struggled into some kind of sitting position.

'Sally?'

'Yes. Hello. What time is it?'

'Sally?'

'Yes. Yes. Hello. David.'

'I must talk to you.'

'Yes. Listen, give me half an hour. OK?'

'Half an hour?'

'Please. I must get my head together.'

'Half an hour it is. Are you all right, sweetie?'

'Fine. I'm fine.'

'Half an hour.'

'Yes.'

I put the phone down. I stared out of the window for a moment or two at the blue sky, at the roofs, at the grey-green hill behind the houses.

Bed is the place to stay, I thought, possibly for ever.

I wondered vaguely why David had called here. Saturday was his golf day.

There was a crash in the garden as a red ball came over the fence.

Laughter.

'Sally.'

I got out of bed.

'Sally, Sally.'

I put my head out of the window.

Hands waved across the fence.

'Good morning,' I called.

'I'm afraid we've . . . um . . .'

'Yes. I can see.'

'Can we . . . um.'

'No, no, no. Give me ten minutes. I'll be down.'

'I could just . . . ummm.'

'No, I'll be down. Ten minutes.'

'Liar, liar, your botttom's on fire.'

'Just shut up and let me get dressed. Go and have your breakfast. Fifteen minutes.'

I went into the bathroom and turned on the taps.

He had left no mess; just gaps where his stuff had been: toothbrush, flannel, shaving things, razor, brush, the little wooden bowl with soap in it, mouthwash; that was pushing it a bit, I thought I bought the last bottle of mouthwash. I dripped some lavender oil into the bath. Pour Hommes, gone. I bet he'd taken the nail scissors, always a bone of contention. I stepped into the bath, just a little too hot, and lowered myself down; I felt my skin reddening as it hit the water, divine agony. I lay back in the scented water and as I did so I caught sight of his dressing gown hanging on the back of the door. I felt the tears coming into my eyes again.

Such nonsense, such bloody nonsense.

Was it my fault?

Did I, as my mother had done, have some invisible notice saying Keep Out. Private. Do not pass beyond this point.

Perhaps we should have had some children.

Now, that was very definitely my fault. I couldn't argue with that; every time the subject came up I had said, 'Next year. Time enough for children later on.' The lure of Pegeen Mike, of Hedda Gabler, Viola, Masha, even Goneril, had been too great for me.

Perhaps you should have your children first, before you are grabbed by ambition, or whatever you'd like to call it. Drag them round the world with you, or hire some kind and wonderful woman to mind them. Then whose children would they be? Yours or hers? Who would they call out for when they fell? To whom would they tell their secrets?

I can answer that.

To no one.

We tell our secrets to no one.

Not even to the beloved of your heart.

* * *

The water settled round me, a cloak of comfort.

'I never thought he would leave me.' I said the words aloud.

I soaped my flannel and scrubbed at my face.

'Never, never,' my mother used to say to me. 'Never, never put soap on your face.'

Scrub.

Scrub away the tears and the exhaustion and the anger. Only soap can do that.

What was the point in being angry anyway?

Anger won't bring him back.

Scrub.

The tension from my back and shoulders.

Scrub.

Scrub, scrub.

David will ring and we will talk about work.

Must work.

My back was aching; my feet felt like lumps of lead.

I could ring him, I thought, at his mother's, or at work, or at . . . No. I could though. I could say please come back and I will stay at home. I will have babies, I will be the perfect wife for you. Here. In this house. I will determine to . . .

Don't be such a fool, Sally. It would be lies, all lies, because even if I were to change like that I would pine. I would no longer be the person I want to be; the person I also thought he wanted me to be.

I will go and see my grandfather.

The thought splintered into my mind and I pushed it away.

I washed my feet.

Grandfather . . .

The last time I had seen him was after my mother's pathetic funeral. I had telephoned him from a call box in the Post Office in Dean's Grange.

His housekeeper had answered the phone.

'The Bishop is busy at the moment. May I take a message?'

'Busy?' I wondered what the hell the old man was at.

'His Grace is writing his memoirs. He doesn't like to be disturbed.'

'This is his granddaughter.'

'I know, miss. Will you give me a message for him?'

'I'd like to come and see him.'

There was a long silence and as I was about to put down the receiver, she spoke again.

'The Bishop would like you to come for dinner tonight. Quarter to eight. And he asked me to say that he retires every night at ten.'

'Well . . .' I was supposed to be meeting Charlie.

'Would that be yes or no?'

'Yes. I'll come. Tell him thank you.'

I thought carefully about what I should wear and decided

on black. Solid funereal black. No touch of colour at all. I
left the Post Office and walked across the road to the car
where Charlie was waiting for me. I told him what I had just
done.

He laughed.

'What a mutt you are, Sal. A glutton for punishment.
You've had a dreadful day, why do this on top of it all?'

'I just thought I should. After all she was his only child.
He must have some feelings for her. And he's my . . . my . . .'

I opened the door and got into the car. He put his hand
gently on my arm.

'Would you like me to come with you? Hunh? Would
that make things easier?'

'No, thanks, darling. I'll be all right. Really I will. Perfectly
all right.'

I put the car into gear. 'I'm going to wear black.'

He laughed again. 'I do love you, Sal, so much.'

That was before we were married.

I had just finished playing Miranda and the mood still
lingered with me: pale, young and innocent.

The black suited me.

My grandfather's house was set in a neat garden, halfway
up the hill of Howth, overlooking Dublin Bay.

I was a few minutes early and I stopped the car at a bend
in the driveway and got out and stood breathing the cool

fresh air. The lights of the city spread like a bright carpet, sweeping down from the hills to the south and west and poking fingers of light into the darkness of the flat lands towards the north. The air was calm and sweet with a hint of autumn dampness in it.

A container vessel was crossing the bay, pulling behind it a wake of glittering waves. I just stood there and looked and breathed very quietly so that I should in no way upset the equilibrium of peace.

Mrs Carruthers opened the hall door and in silence I followed her across the hall to my grandfather's study.

It must have been about three years since I had seen him, just after the death of my grandmother. He seemed to have grown smaller in every way. He sat in a large chair by the fire holding a glass of pale sherry in his arthritic hand. He didn't get up when I came into the room, just gestured with his hand towards a chair on the other side of the fireplace with a slight movement of his head. I sat down and Mrs Carruthers placed a glass of sherry on the small table beside me.

'Thank you.' My voice sounded alarmingly loud. 'Good evening, Grandfather.'

He didn't speak until after she had left the room and closed the door.

Apart from his purple shirt and white dog collar he also

was dressed in black. Even his hair was black, wavy and strong, flowing back from his forehead in thick ripples. I wondered if he dyed it.

'Good evening,' he said at last.

There was a long silence.

I sipped at my sherry.

The fire crackled.

'I did not attend the funeral.'

'I noticed.'

'I was afraid that my presence might embarrass whatever clergyman . . .'

'She said no God. She left a note saying no God. So . . .'

'I see. No God?'

'Yes.'

He thought about that for a long silent time.

He tipped the remains of the sherry into his mouth.

'No God. It is quite difficult to arrange a funeral without some God or other.'

I shrugged. 'The undertaker did it all. We put her in the family plot. Dean's Grange. I presume that was the right thing to do?'

He frowned. 'What a pity she felt she had to leave such a note.'

I opened my bag and began to search for the piece of paper but he waved his hand.

'I don't want to see it,' he said.

At this moment Mrs Carruthers opened the door and announced that dinner was on the table.

He jumped to his feet with amazing alacrity. He was wearing black velvet slippers with his initials embroidered in gold.

'Cool,' I muttered.

He sped across the room and out of the door.

I followed him.

The dining room was high and dark. Only the table was lit. I wondered if he ate with such formality every night, or had this been arranged specially for me.

The walls were weighted with portraits, men and women gazed through the darkness at us as we took our seats; maybe, of course, it was for their entertainment that he sat each evening in this show of light and ate his dinner in silence. Their eyes certainly watched us.

He stood by his chair, his head bowed; I also stood by my chair, head also bowed and waited. I felt the eyes of the dead penetrating my skull.

'*Benedictus, benedicat, per Iesum Christum Dominum Nostrum.*'

We pulled out our chairs and sat.

'One day,' I said cheerfully, 'it would be very kind if you were to tell me who all these people are.'

'I do not see the need.'

There was a long pause during which I wondered what I should say.

'They are my ancestors.'

'And also mine, Grandfather.'

He acknowledged this truth with a regretful nod of his head.

'Wouldn't it be a good thing if somebody else knew about them? If there were someone else to remember them?'

He pushed a bottle of Bordeaux towards me and indicated that I should help myself.

I poured a little into my glass; my hand was trembling.

'What is the use of remembering?'

'Maybe it is of no importance to you, but . . .'

'I am not saying that it is of no importance to me. I am just asking you what use you think it is to you or anybody else. Anybody.'

'If there's stuff you're not allowed to know it takes on a giant significance. I'd like to be allowed to know . . . even a little. I have no background. I grow from secrets. I hate that. There is little feeding in other people's secrets. That lady there for instance.' I nodded towards a lady in green on the wall above his head.

'Ah,' he said. He spread a large damask napkin across his knees and then picked up his spoon. He held it poised above the avocado pear, which sat, stuffed with prawns and a sauce that I bet did not come from Marks & Spencer, on a plate in front of him.

'Ah,' he said again.

Neatly he scooped some pear onto his spoon and popped it into his mouth. 'Ah.' He patted at his mouth with his napkin.

'My mother's mother.'

'My great-great-grandmother.'

'She was an O'Hara.'

Another spoonful of avocado.

'From County Sligo.'

I leant towards him. 'Grandfather, you must help me. I really need to find a family for myself. I really, really need to find my father.'

His face closed, a dark and final closure. 'Eat your dinner.'

I began to eat.

We both ate in silence.

After a while, as Mrs Carruthers moved our plates and replaced them with others, I pulled myself together.

'I'm sorry for bothering you like this, but we are alone now . . . at least I am alone. You have these, the dead. I had only Mother and she wasn't a whole person at all . . . and I have you. And you . . . have me. For what that's worth. Grandfather.'

I touched his hand.

He flinched.

'I'm sorry,' I said.

'I'd really like to have a family. I don't need to love them . . . just . . . know they're there. Please.'

'It is not possible.' Having spoken those cruel words he suddenly gave me a very charming smile. 'I saw your Miranda.'

That startled me.

'You . . .'

'Yes. I saw it. I did think you were remarkably good. I thought you caught her limpid innocence very well. You didn't play her as stupid. Some actresses do that. She wasn't stupid. She was astonishingly innocent. Her father had never told her anything, taught her anything about the world . . . the real evil world, that is. Never.'

'I'm glad you enjoyed the show.'

'Not so much the show as your performance.' He closed his eyes.

> 'Now my charms are all o'erthrown,
> And what strength I have's mine own;
> Which is most faint. Now 'tis true
> I must be here confin'd by you,
> Or sent to Naples.'

His voice was rich and low; his eyes remained closed. He sounded like a man much younger than his years.

> *'Let me not,*
> *Since I have my dukedom got*
> *And pardoned the deceiver, dwell*
> *In this bare island by your spell,*
> *But release me from my bands*
> *With the help of your good hands.'*

His voice faltered and then stopped. He opened his eyes.

'Good hands,' he repeated. He looked for a moment bewildered.

'Gentle breath . . .' I prompted. He smiled briefly.

> *'. . . of yours my sails*
> *Must fill, or else my project fails,*
> *Which way to please. Now I want*
> *Spirits to enforce, art to enchant;*
> *And my ending is despair*
> *Unless I be relieved by prayer,*
> *Which pierces so that it assaults*
> *Mercy itself, and frees all faults.*
> *As you from crimes would pardoned be,*
> *Let your indulgence set me free.'*

The silence was long.

Then.

I clapped.

He bowed his head.

'That was wonderful. It really was.'

'I played Prospero in school.' Then he said after a long pause, 'I remembered my lines.'

'I would love to have seen you.'

'It was a long time ago. I was seventeen. I was very good. Yes.'

His voice faded away. He picked up his knife and fork and began to eat.

'You only forgot one word. After so many years, I . . .'

'We will not speak about it any more. No more.'

We ate in another silence.

I tried to visualise him as Prospero.

All those years ago, stern, old, only of course he wasn't old, only old in the eyes of his audience; the colonial overlord, the spell master, definitely old for all those watching seventeen-year-olds.

The food was delicious. I watched his face as he savoured it.

After a long time he spoke again.

'We are all alone, you know. Each one of us. If you have God, His love will keep you warm. That is what they say.'

'Grandfather . . .'

'If you don't have God your very bones must be cold. I feel sad your mother did not feel His warmth.'

Fucking old bastard, I thought.

'I'm not cold. I'm not lonely. I have friends. I have work. I don't feel the need for God. I just want to know who the hell I am. She certainly needed something to keep her warm, I'll give you that. Her life was a misery. I'll give you that too. I don't think it was anything to do with God. I think it was something to do with you and Grandma. I'd like you to tell me . . .'

'Tell you what?'

'Everything. I want to know everything. I have a right to know . . .'

'No.' He put his knife and fork down on his plate and leant forward to pick up a small silver bell. 'No rights. You have no rights to knowledge that your mother kept from you.' He rang the bell. 'None whatsoever.'

The door opened and Mrs Carruthers came in. I wondered if she had been standing outside, listening.

He made a tiny gesture towards me with his right hand. 'Miss Sarah has to go.'

'Grandfather . . .'

'Now.'

The housekeeper was holding the door.

I stood up. 'You are an impossible old man.'

He bowed his head as if he were thanking me.

I walked towards the door.

The men and women on the walls followed me with their eyes.

Mrs Carruthers stared at the floor.

At the door I paused. 'My mother was buried today. I thought under circumstances . . .'

'Goodnight, granddaughter.'

'I'll be back.'

The housekeeper came down the hall after me and opened the front door. I stepped out into the autumn night; there was a hint of turf smoke in the air.

'Goodnight,' I said to no one in particular.

'Goodnight,' and then the click of the door closing.

* * *

The scrubbing was over.

I was dry and dressed when the phone rang again.

'Yes.'

'Half an hour, doll. Feeling better?'

'Good morning, David.' I made my voice sound sprightly. 'Why aren't you heading for the golf course?'

'Never heard of mobiles? Are you bathed? In your full health and strength?'

'You'll be arrested.'

'My lovely wife is driving.'

'Say hi from me. Couldn't we leave this till Monday?'

'Not really. They're being pressured by New York and they tell me you won't go. Is that true?'

'That's true. That's what I told them.'

'Why didn't you talk to me about this before you said a thing like that to them. How many times have I said to you, if you keep a dog you don't need to do the barking? Hunh? They want you. They're prepared to pay.'

'No.' I mumbled the word.

'What?'

'I said, no. I can't get back on the stage and play that part again. I'm sick sick sick of Pegeen Mike. And I don't want to talk about it now. For God's sake, David, go and play golf.'

His wife said something to him that I couldn't hear.

'Monday,' I said. 'I promise, Monday. I'll talk to you about it then.'

'Think about being the toast of New York.'

'No.'

'What's wrong with you?'

'Charlie's left me.'

'What?'

'He's gone. Last night. So please ring me back on Monday. Leave me alone now.'

'Come off it, baby. This can't be true. You're pulling my leg.'

His wife said something again and he squawked at her.

'You're cracking up,' I shouted down the phone and put down the receiver.

Phew.

Monday.

My new life would begin on Monday.

For now I had no father.

I had no mother.

I probably didn't have an agent.

I had no husband, no children, not even a dog.

If I had a dog I could put my face on its soft neck and it would lick my cheek. I would like that comfort.

I would like almost any comfort at this moment.

Perhaps I could borrow a dog.

The thought made me smile.

Then, someone was knocking on the door.

That wiped the smile off my face.

I went downstairs. It was my next-door neighbour. I could see her silhouette through the glass in the door. I hated that glass door; for years I had been meaning to replace it with a solid one. I must do that on Monday, I thought, the beginning of my new life.

I opened the door.

Jenny and I stared at each other in silence for a moment and then she brushed past me into the hall. She was wearing a track suit and bedroom slippers. In her hand she held a piece of paper.

'Hi.' We both said the word simultaneously.

Jenny moved towards the kitchen. 'I know,' she said, waving the paper. 'He shoved this through the letter box sometime or other. We live so close, Sal, it's difficult not to know an awful lot about your neighbours.' She put the paper down on the table and turned on the tap. 'I'm making coffee. Read it.'

I picked it up and looked at it. Charlie's writing, that was for sure.

'Would you rather have tea?'

'No. Coffee's great.'

Dear J, pop in and see if Sal is OK. She has thrown me out. C.

'Short and sweet,' said Jenny.

'I did not throw the bastard out.'

'Mummy!'

Jenny switched on the kettle.

'Mama. Mummy.'

'Bloody kids.' She opened the door into the garden. 'What the hell is it?'

'I did not throw the bastard out.'

'Throw us over the ball.'

'Can I not have ten minutes' peace?'

'I did not throw the bastard out.' I shouted the words after her. I leant against the door and began to laugh.

'Where is it?'

'Under that tree. Yes. There.'

Jenny picked up the muddy ball and looked at it with distaste.

'Mummummummy.'

'If I give it to you please, please, please, don't kick it over here again.'

'Come on, Mum. Throw it back.'

She threw the ball over the fence and wiped her hands on her trousers.

She walked past me into the kitchen. I was still laughing.

'So, it's funny?'

I shook my head. 'I'm just laughing. If I didn't laugh I'd cry. I'm sick of crying. I did not throw him out. He has such a bloody nerve. I swear to God it was after he said that he was leaving me . . . when it suited him. He was leaving me. So . . .'

The kettle boiled.

'I just said now. You must go now.'

Jenny was spooning coffee into the pot. 'Are you quite sure he meant what he said?'

'I am leaving you. He said it several times. Just in case.'

'In case of what?'

'In case I didn't understand.'

Jenny poured the boiling water into the coffee pot; the smell filled the room. I took a deep breath; the smell filled my body.

'He couldn't have put it more plainly.'

'What did you do?'

'I threw my coffee at him.'

Jenny laughed. 'That's the stuff to give the troops,' she said.

She put two brightly coloured mugs on the table; one was orange, the other, yellow.

'Then his. That was overkill, I admit. But there's something quite fun about throwing coffee at people. He was furious.'

'I bet.'

She put the coffee pot on the table and sat down. She pulled a pack of cigarettes and a lighter from her pocket. She held the pack out towards me.

'Cig?'

'No.'

'Mind if I do?'

She didn't wait for an answer; she stuck a cigarette in her mouth and lit it. She took a long drag, swallowing the smoke deep inside her. I pushed down the plunger in the coffee pot and filled both mugs. The smoke inside Jenny slowly drifted out into the kitchen again and hung above her head like a feather.

'Do you know about Marianna?'

'All of them. All the Mariannas and Joans and Annies. Yes.'

'Nobody ever knows how much a wife knows or wants to know. Flashes in the pan. Each one. That's what I think anyway.'

'But now he's gone.'

'He's going to want back.'

I shook my head. 'No. After Marianna it will be someone else. And on and on. It's partly my fault. It does take two to tango. I realise that. But it's not all my fault.' I thought about faults and all that jazz for quite a while. 'No. I do love him. I could cope with him when he just fucked about and presumed I didn't know anything, but now I don't . . .' Bloody tears choked me.

'He's a bastard.' Smoke trickled from Jenny's mouth as she spoke.

I laughed. 'Let's be honest, fair and square; I'm the real bastard in this house. One and only. Always have been.'

'For God's sake, Sal, who cares about that sort of thing?'

'I do. I always have.'

She put out a hand and touched my neck. I shrugged her hand away.

'Don't be too nice to me. I might bawl. I really feel like bawling, but I'm sick of it.'

'Sally . . .'

'For years I've cried. I've been moody, grumpy, really unpredictable. He was great. He always got me out of it. Blackness. I don't know what I'll do without him. I wouldn't have children. I kept saying next year. Not just yet. Some time. I never said never, but he knew that was what I meant. Yes. He knew. It's a bloody world, isn't it.'

'It's the way you make it.'

'You know my mother killed herself?'

'No. I . . .'

'Yes. Six months before Charlie and I were married. Just quite out of the blue. She took an overdose.'

'I'm sorry.'

'It's not something I talk about. I suppose she couldn't stand being alive any longer. Alone. She was always alone. She had me, of course, but I kept going away from her. I couldn't bear the burden of her clinging to me, pulling me down. I get so frightened. I can see the same thing happening to me. Sometimes, only sometimes. Most of the time I'm OK.'

'You mustn't think like that. You've got your work. You've got loads of friends and he'll be back.'

The doorbell rang.

'Oh God!'

'I'll go.' Jenny jumped up and, trailing smoke after her, went to answer the door. I listened to voices rising and falling. Not concerning me, seemingly.

I poured myself some more coffee. I didn't want it. It was just something to do. The very thought of letting it slip down my throat made me feel ill.

The voices rose and fell.

I stared at my coffee cup.

Jenny laughed.

The hall door closed. She came back into the room and sat down. She reached for the cigarettes.

'Men,' she said after a moment. 'Don to be exact. He came to remind me that his parents are coming to dinner tonight. As if.' She lit her cigarette. 'As bloody if. Shopping is on his mind. Take the kids and go and shop, I said. There's a list on the kitchen table. For fuck's sake he can shop, can't he? Dress the kids I said. He'd take them in their pyjamas. He honestly would. And make the beds before you go. I said that too. My mother-in-law will need to know that the children's beds are made. Even on Saturday.' She gave a little burst of laughter. She leant towards me, taking care not to touch me. 'Talk.'

'I must lie down where all the ladders start,
In the foul rag-and-bone shop of the heart'

'No,' she said. 'Never lie down. And Yeats was a portentous old fool. At least that's what I have always thought.'

I smiled. I wondered if she meant pretentious. Probably not.

'I went to the Custom House. That was where you used to have to go to find your birth certificate. Years ago. Eighteen, I must have been. I probably needed a passport. She didn't want me to go. She did everything she could to stop me. She had never let me go on school trips or away with friends. I always thought it was money, but money was no problem. She just didn't want me to see that damn certificate. Anyway there it was written officially . . . father unknown. It gave me such a fright although . . . well, it was what she'd always said. "You have no father." I went home and asked her again. I showed her the certificate. I shoved it under her nose. "You don't need to know," she yelled at me. But I needed. I really did. I still do.'

'There's not much point,' said Jenny.

'You couldn't possibly know. I'm half a person. I can tell you it's horrible. Believe me. Father unknown. All I ever wanted to know was his name. I didn't want to go and pester him. No. Nothing like that. Just to know his name.

After all it should be my name too. Maybe this is all quite
unreasonable, but it's what I am. Perhaps I only forget when
I'm acting, being some totally other person. Do you think
I'm mad?'

'I . . .'

'Don't say anything. There isn't anything I haven't already
said inside my head. I have argued with my unreason for
years. Got nowhere. Charlie was good. He used to buck me
up when I was really down. I suppose he needed a bit of
peace, someone new, someone he didn't have to keep
reassuring. I can see it must be tiring to have to keep
reassuring someone.'

'Your mother . . .'

'Poor old Moth. God, she was such a pain. I used to hate
her. That's quite normal though. I bet you hated your mother
from time to time. Everyone does. She used to drink like a
fish, especially in the years before she . . . When I was grown
up and didn't need her attention all the time. But even then,
even when she was almost unconscious, she never let slip his
name. I used to try and trick her into it. Poor bloody
woman.'

We sat for a long time in silence. Strangely I felt better;
my head was clearing.

'I used to call her Moth,' I said eventually.

'It's a good name to call your mother. I like Moth. My

mother was very unmothlike.' Jenny's hand gestured hugeness in the air. 'She was so orderly. Everything had its place. Nothing was allowed to stray. I used to hate her for that. She used to inspect our homework, it never mattered if it was right or wrong, it had to be tidy. Look at me now. I married the untidiest man I could find and we live in pigsty heaven. And he's a Prod. A so-called Prod. I thought she would die when I did that. At least we got married; nobody bothers any longer. How she would have raged if we had been so untidy as to have four kids and no wedding ring, no christenings. Even Prod christenings were better than no christenings as far as she was concerned.' She threw her head back and laughed, then she jumped from her seat and threw her arms around me, a warm and most loving gesture. We remained clenched together for a while, then she loosed her hold and went back to her seat.

'I think,' I said to her, 'you should go. Go and shop with Don. I'm all right now, really I am. I'm going to go and see Grandfather. Thank you. You're a good friend. I hope you will always be my friend.'

'Yup.' She smiled. 'I'd better go and shop. He would scramble my list. Bring home all the wrong things. Any time you need me, just whistle.' She got up and moved towards the door. 'I'm sorry about the kids and the football and all that sort of stuff.'

'None of that matters.'

' 'Bye.'

'Bye. Have a good time with your mother-in-law.'

'Yee haw.' She was gone.

The room smelled of smoke.

The war, I thought. I'd better have a look before doing anything else. Put things in perspective. Perspective slides.

I pressed the button and immediately was in Baghdad. Rageh Omaar stood on a roof somewhere and the sky flashed behind him. You could of course, I thought to myself, set this all up electronically. It doesn't have to be true. Where does that leave perspective?

A thick cloud of smoke and dust made it seem like night-time. He was quite chirpy though; his eyes looked anxious but his mouth smiled a little white smile. Some huge trucks rumbled along a dusty road, GIs grinned at the camera. Rageh Omaar's voice chirped away. I didn't want to hear what he was saying so I switched off the set. So much for perspective!

* * *

Seamus, at the stage door, had stopped me as I had been leaving a rehearsal. 'You're to ring your mam,' he shouted at me. He always shouted.

'My . . .?'

'Mam. She needs you to ring her asap.'

'Oh God, what's the matter with her.'

'She just said you were to ring her. She sounded upset like.'

I rummaged in my bag.

No change.

I never have change when I need it.

Seamus pushed open the door to his cubbyhole.

'Come on in. You can use mine.'

'Thanks.'

He stood up and let me sit at his desk.

An electric fan heater blew hot air up my skirt.

Moth must have been standing by the phone.

'Sally.' She spoke before I did.

'Moth . . .'

'The Bishop's wife is dying.' She never used the word mother.

She sounded as if she had been crying.

'Where is she?'

'Vincent's. Mrs Carruthers telephoned about half an hour ago. I didn't even know she was ill.'

'I'll go home and get the car. Then I'll be straight over to you.'

'I didn't mean to disturb you. I . . . I . . . I just thought . . .'

'I'll be as quick as I can. 'Bye darling.'

I put down the receiver and sat looking across the table at a picture of Christ holding his heart between his widespread fingers.

I turned to Seamus. 'Do you believe in God?'

He was startled by my question. 'Of course.'

I stood up. 'You're a lucky man.'

'I was born believing in God and I expect you were too.'

'No. No. No. Nothing like that at all. My mother used to laugh when anyone mentioned his name. I never learnt to say God bless Mummy and . . . Perhaps I was lucky. I do try to work things out.' I moved to the door. 'Sorry. Things flood into my mind from time to time. I'd better dash. My grandmother is dying. Thank you, Seamus.' I stepped out into the windy lane. People were pushing and shoving, eager to get home, or anyway out of the wind. They clutched their coats around them, their handbags and parcels, their hair lifted with the sharp wind.

I tried to imagine the old woman dying in her hospital bed, shrunk almost to nothing. All I had seen were photographs in Moth's room, a rather austere face she had, but young, with hair piled up on her head and a long nose. Many years ago that had been, pre bishoprics, pre all the formalities that go with such elevation, pre me. Definitely pre me.

I wondered if, on those few occasions that Moth had

taken me to the house and left me outside sitting in the car, that woman had peeped through half-closed curtains or opened the hall door just a crack in order to see me.

I didn't think so; hers had not been the face of a peeper. What had she thought about me, that she couldn't bring herself to even give me a passing glance? How could she be so afraid of seeing me?

I would so love my life to be simple, just like everyone else's seems to be. To act and then to sleep; that seems like the best way of living that I can think of. Learn lines, move, speak with many tongues, borrow the tears and laughter of others and then when it is all over go home and sleep.

After applause.

I do have to say I like applause.

There were taxis in the rank. I slipped into one and gave the driver my address. When we got home I stepped straight into my car which was sitting in the driveway. I wasted no time.

Moth was standing in the hall when I arrived. The light was on and I could see her through the glass panel, leaning against the banisters clutching her coat around her, like someone waiting for a train that might never arrive. She opened the door when she heard the car pulling up outside the house and was down the path before I had time to turn off the engine.

'I was waiting.' She whispered the words as she opened the door and got into the car.

'I came as quickly as I could.'

I leant towards her and kissed her cheek. 'I'm sorry, Moth, really sorry.'

My mother became a torrent of tears. They splashed through her fingers and ran down her cheeks and neck; she was unable to speak.

'Here.' I snatched a bundle of Kleenex from the door pocket and shoved them into her hand. 'Here. Here.'

I put the car in gear and began to drive towards St Vincent's hospital.

After a while her sobbing became less frenzied; she began to pull herself together. 'So long ago. We were happy. I remember being happy. A child. Yes. It comes back. That loss. That loss of happiness.' She was hiccuping between each group of words. 'I know she won't see me. I know she ... I have to go. Yes. Maybe she'll ...' Her voice petered out. She blew her nose fiercely.

'She'll what?' I asked.

'I don't know. Want me to be there. Smile at me, perhaps. Forgive me.'

'Forgive you? For what in God's name? You should be forgiving her.'

'I don't want her to die hating me.'

'I don't suppose she'll do that. Here. Take some more of these.' I pushed the Kleenex box towards her. She ignored it. 'Dear Moth, how could anyone hate you?'

You're too pathetic to be hated, I thought, except of course by me.

'She could.' She sniffed and then took another handful of tissues. 'They expected so much from me. They . . . she had put so much energy and, I suppose, love into bringing me up and then.' The tears had started again, rolling down her cheeks. 'I let them down. I let the Bishop down. I think that was what she hated most. She adored him you know. And . . . and . . . and . . .'

I stopped at red lights and looked out of the window. I didn't know whether to speak or remain silent. I chose silence. It seemed easier. The man in the car next to me was tapping impatiently with his finger on the steering wheel; I caught his eye and smiled at him. He looked away quickly; idiot, I thought, a smile would have cost him nothing.

'Of course he wasn't a bishop then, but they couldn't have borne scandal. They never wanted that in their lives. Who wants scandal? We all know the answer to that.'

The lights changed and I shot off ahead of the man who wouldn't smile.

Moth opened the top of her window and pushed out a wodge of Kleenex.

'Moth,' I said angrily. 'That is such a horrid thing to do.'

'Sorry. I'm so sorry.' The tears came even harder. 'I'm really sorry. I didn't . . .'

'Apart from the fact that it is seriously ungreen. I could get fined, so I could, if we were caught.'

'What's ungreen?'

'Oh for heaven's sake. I suppose I was the scandal.'

She didn't answer. I swung through the gates of the hospital car park.

'What do you want me to do? Come in with you? Hang about? Go home?'

'Wait here, Sally, please wait.'

I turned into a space.

'All right. I'll be here. I've got my script. I can work. If I need a cup of coffee I'll go into the hospital. Or the loo. But just wait here, I'll be back.' I kissed her. 'Don't fret, darling. Take these with you.' I clamped her hand round the box of Kleenex and gently pushed her out of the car.

* * *

I remember it now with such clarity.

It is like a film in my mind, clear, in colour, quite unequivocally, my past.

I am startled by the recollection; for heaven's sake, I can't remember the day before yesterday, so how do I manage to remember the face of the man in the next car to me, those years ago.

What spotlight in the mind shines on these scenes?

It was St Joan I was working on.

My first really big role. Huge. I must call it huge.

And so bloody exciting.

I felt sick most of the time. I remember that well.

Nerves.

I did not need Moth's problems on my back as well as Joan of Arc's.

It is an old saying, that he who tells too much truth is sure to be hanged.

Yes. I remember those words coming into my mind as I sat in the car that evening.

I laughed.

God does not allow the whole truth to be told.

Yes. I laughed.

I suppose some people might call me a heartless bitch.

I was sorry for Moth, there was no question about that, sorry with all my heart for her.

But not the other, the old dying one.

Nor for the Bishop, God's man. No sorrow there.

I remember those thoughts in my head.

I sat with my book on my knee and learned Shaw's lines.

God does not allow the whole truth to be told.

My thoughts wandered to Charlie, who I thought I might be beginning to love. I wondered if he could carry me and my burden on his back.

Forever.

Big word.

Big burden to carry half a person.

* * *

Once, last year in some black mood, I had banged my head against the sitting-room wall until I fell bruised and exhausted onto the floor.

'What the hell was that about?' Charlie asked me. I was on the sofa then wrapped in rugs and he was holding a cloth soaked in cold water against my forehead. His face was pale. I tried to smile at him.

'It's OK. Honestly it is. It's years since I did anything like that. I'm really, really sorry.'

'Why?' he asked me again.

I said nothing.

'Why? You must tell me, Sally. We're married. You have to tell me why. It will help. You should have no secrets from me, but you have.'

I shook my painful head.

'There's no use pretending that you haven't.'

'No.'

He sighed. 'I can't bear it when you shut me out. You make me feel so helpless. I feel as if you hate me for some reason.'

'Oh no. I love you.'

I shut my eyes and lied.

'It's work. We're having a rotten time at rehearsals. We're all on edge. I'm sorry. It won't happen again. I promise.'

He stared at me. I felt my face going red.

He got up from the sofa, removing his warmth from me and the cold compress from my forehead.

'Be like that,' he said and left the room.

* * *

It is my fault that he left me. I know that. Those other ladies tell him their secrets. He needs that; as far as he is concerned that is what love is about. He likes the feeling of security it gives him. I tell you my secrets, you tell me yours and by some magic we are bound together. His eyes lure people into confidential talk and the velvet of his voice. Moth liked him, but she also thought he was not the right man for me.

'You'll drive him away,' she said to me once. 'With your moods and your scowlings.'

How right she'd been.

How bloody, bloody, bloody right.

* * *

I had fallen asleep.

Head lurched against the window. Crick in the neck.

St Joan had slipped from my hand to the floor.

Moth was banging on the glass.

It took me a moment or two to remember where I was.

'Moth! Oh yes.' I leant over and opened the door for her.
She slumped into the seat.

'It's over.' She slammed the door. 'Over.'

I looked for the box of tissues. It was on the floor with
St Joan. Moth wasn't crying; she was very pale, ghost-
coloured, but her eyes were dry.

'Should we offer to drive the Bishop home? What do you
think?'

I sighed. 'It's up to you.'

'Perhaps we should. He looked so . . . so . . .' Her voice
trailed away. She put out her hand and opened the door.
'. . . very tired and old. Yes. Old and very tired. Should I?'

'For God's sake, Moth, go and ask him. Stop beating
about the bush. What time is it anyway?'

Moth shook her head.

I looked at my watch. 'Half past nine.'

Three hours I had been sitting in that car. No wonder I'd
fallen asleep.

'Well?' I almost shouted at her. 'What do you want to do?'

'We'll go.' She shut the door. 'Just go, Sally. I'm sure he'll be all right. Mrs Carruthers . . . someone. Just go.'

I put the car into gear and drove off.

'Will you come home and spend the night?'

I thought for a moment or two and then nodded.

'I'll have to leave very early in the morning though.'

'That's all right. I wouldn't expect you to do anything else. No. No.' Her voice petered out. She smiled briefly at me. 'Hauntings. Things like that; they don't happen when there's someone else around.'

'Hauntings? Moth, don't be stupid.'

'I do not want to be haunted by her.'

'Well, hauntings or no hauntings I am only staying the one night.'

I had a sudden vision of being sucked back in there for ever.

And ever.

And ever.

'That's quite clear. As I said I wouldn't expect . . .' She stared at me and her eyes began to fill with tears once more.

I patted her hand and turned the key in the ignition.

'I would not expect . . .'

'Did she speak to you, Moth? Was she . . . was she . . .?'

'She looked at me. Straight at me . . . and then . . .'

'What?'

There was a very long pause.

'She shut her eyes. Like she was pulling the blinds down and she died. Just like that. She died.'

'Oh darling Moth.'

'Suppose it was only to be expected. It was . . . How old are you?'

'Thirty-two.'

'She hasn't spoken one word to me in thirty-two years. I was seventeen then, now I'm forty-nine. I've been a mother for such a long time.'

'Moth . . .'

'No,' she said. 'I have always said no. I'll always say no. You have no father.'

Bugger, I thought. Bugger.

'Drive home,' she said.

She clenched her hands on her knees.

I began to drive.

We drove in silence to Moth's house.

*　*　*

Yes.

Perspective.

The word flickered in my head.

What on earth good were Shakespeare, Chekhov, Beckett during our moments of consternation?

Or indeed during the world's moments of consternation? They recorded. So did Rageh Omaar, John Simpson, Charlie Bird.

I suppose the recorders are necessary, so that things don't get out of hand.

But the murders in the night still go on. Graves are dug, the innocent bodies of children are thrown into the holes. Oedipus eyes continue to bleed and what do I do? Bloody hell . . . I'm not even waiting for Godot. I don't even have that excuse. I sleep and my dreams become nightmares. Nightmares of such infinitesimal importance to anyone other than myself, and possibly the father for whom I long, that I spend my life in a state of embarrassment. My mother commits suicide; at least she did something. My husband leaves me, because I refuse to bring children into this terrifying world.

I refuse. I suppose that might be considered to be a statement of some sort.

I just act.

The very act of acting being a form of sleep.

Act.

The maggot.

Yes.

And watch.

The children on the television with their brown frightened and accusing eyes, they may be dead tomorrow and

I

will

still

be acting

the maggot.

*   *   *

Grandfather's face came into my mind and his shadowy voice sounded.

'Now my charms are all o'erthrown'.

Oh grandfather, what an old bastard you are.

'And what strength I have's mine own.'

But you are my old bastard. We are the only ones left.

That I know of anyway.

Maybe he'll leave me his not inconsiderable fortune.

Now there's a thought.

A thought that made me laugh, and the laugh sent a surge of energy through me.

What do bishops do on Saturday?

I shall go and find out.

Interrupt his prayers perhaps?

I think not.

He's never seemed the praying sort to me.

Maybe he spends Saturday in bed.

Anyway I bet I'll surprise him.

I ran down the stairs and snatched up my bag from the hall table. My keys, my sunglasses, some money just in case of emergencies.

I noticed that Charlie had forgotten the two pictures of the school rugby team that had always hung in the hall. He smiled proudly at me from the front row. I smiled politely back.

The sun was warm and one of my neighbour's murderous cats slept on the bonnet of my car. I scratched the top of its head and it opened a large yellow eye and looked at me.

'Scoot,' I said. It flicked its tail and shut its eye again.

'You silly bugger.' I picked it up and placed it on the wall between the two houses.

The cat sighed.

'Mmmrp.'

I got into the car and slammed the door and then remembered that I had done nothing about having the locks changed.

Story of my life.

I rolled the window down and spoke to the cat, the only living creature around at that moment.

'Mind the house for me. Don't let anyone in. Anyone.'

The cat yawned, showing its killer teeth and its delicately

curled pink tongue. It turned away from me and jumped down into its own garden.

So much for cats.

One day I must get one.

*　*　*

I got cold feet as I turned in through the Bishop's gate.

'Excelsior,' I muttered as I put my foot on the accelerator.

The windows on each side of the door glittered in the sun; the knocker had been polished to within an inch of its life.

I rang the bell and waited, nervously jiggling my keys in my hand. Maybe I'd need to make a quick getaway.

I heard soft footsteps cross the hall. The door opened and Mrs Carruthers stood there.

'Good morning.'

'Miss,' said the housekeeper.

'I've come to see the Bishop. Is he in?'

'If you would wait until . . .' The door was closing. I did a quickstep that brought me into the hall. I smiled cheerfully at Mrs Carruthers.

'I should have said grandfather, shouldn't I? I'll wait here until you tell him.'

Mrs Carruthers turned and walked away from me across the sunstriped hall.

'I don't want lunch or anything. I just want to see him,' I called softly after her.

She gave no sign that she had heard me, just walked across the hall and along the passage.

It was a long time before she came back.

My heart failed me.

I wondered should I slip out the door.

I rattled my keys.

I sang a little song.

Finally I sat myself down on a scroll-back chair.

I heard her feet returning.

'He says ten minutes. He'll see you for ten . . .'

'Thanks,' I said. I stood up and followed her back to the sitting room where he and I had met the first time I visited him.

He was sitting at a desk near the window.

I walked past Mrs Carruthers to the centre of the room.

'Good morning, Grandfather.'

'What do you want?'

He didn't turn to face me, he stared out of the window across the bay towards Dublin.

'I just needed to see you.'

'Needed?'

'Yes.'

He sighed.

He stood up and turned round.

He looked tired and fierce, mostly tired.

I wondered how long he had.

'Why?' he asked. 'There is nothing I can do for you.'

'Perhaps I can do something for you, though.'

He laughed. 'I hardly think so.'

I moved towards him and put my hand out to touch his shoulder.

He allowed me to do that. His jacket was soft velvet. Black, of course.

'I'd really like to come and visit you. We could read to each other, if you didn't want to talk. Or just sit silently. Once a week. I'd like to do that.' I waited a long time for him to answer, my hand perched on his velvet shoulder. 'I'd really like that.'

'I do not want you coming here.'

'I want to come.'

He shrugged.

My hand fell from his shoulder.

'We could talk about *The Tempest*. Or the work that you are doing. I'm sure you would like to air your views to someone rather than Mrs Carruthers.'

'I have a secretary. I have a researcher. I am quite able to air my views, thank you. My memoirs are after all my memoirs. You will be able to read them when I am dead. I have lived in interesting times. They will be my public memoirs. The rest will die with me.'

'Grandfather . . .'

'I know why you want to come here and pry into my life. I do not want you searching through my secrets, my hates, my sorrows.'

'But you're wrong. I promise you . . . I promise I won't do any of those things. I just want to be with you. You could hold my hand from time to time. My husband has left me. I need a rock. Couldn't you . . .'

'You want me to be a rock?'

He sounded surprised.

'Yes.'

He laughed. 'Tell me, why did your husband leave you?'

'I'm trying to work it out. I thought we were OK. Rather good actually. But I didn't want to have children. I didn't think he minded. I think he thought I didn't love him. I think he hated my secrets.' I stopped and gave a little laugh. 'But then so do I. I hate the secrets I know nothing about, other people's secrets, that have upset my life. I'm a bit weird. I didn't think he minded that either. He was a rock. I felt that every time things were bad he . . . oh hell. I need a rock, Grandfather. Moth didn't have one and look what happened to her.'

'I think you can go now. I've had enough of your carry-on.' He went and sat down again at his desk, his back firmly towards me. 'Go.'

'I think you ought to consider my suggestion.'

'I think you should go.'

'All right, but I promise you I'll be coming back.'

He didn't speak.

'We should try to like each other,' I said and left the room.

No Mrs Carruthers this time, so I let myself out into the garden's sunshine.

I would be very hard pushed to like him, I thought.

I closed the door gently behind me, got into the car and drove home.

* * *

I passed the rest of the weekend pigging out in front of the television, alone, watching the war.

'America has entered a fierce struggle to save the world.' I learnt that. I got up and fetched a rug and wrapped myself in it. My house seemed cold and empty. No one telephoned. No one called to see me. I just ate chocolates and lived with Nick Witchell, Gavin Hewett, Nick Gowing and of course Charlie Bird. All wearing flak jackets.

'We are telling you the truth,' they say with their mouths and their eyes. 'That is our mission.'

Rubble, children, distraught women clutching their scarves across their faces, their eyes filled with grief and rage.

They give birth astride of a grave, the light gleams an instant, then it's night once more.

I made myself hot black coffee and watched once more wrapped in my mother's cashmere rug.

After a while I got up and looked for my copy of *Waiting for Godot*. I turned off the TV and spent the rest of the day reading and rereading the play.

* * *

Monday it was raining.

No children kicking ball.

The sound of the Hoover purring through the party wall.

This was the beginning of my new life.

It seemed much the same as the old one.

Get up.

Have a bath.

Brush your teeth.

Get dressed.

Key in the door. There you are, like clockwork.

'Howaya. Sally.'

'Good morning, Mrs Murdoch. I hope you had a good weekend.'

She shook her umbrella out of the hall door and left it
open on the doorstep. Threw her raincoat onto the end of
the banisters. She waddled into the kitchen and put on the
kettle. Never start work without a cup of tea.

'Took the kids to the ah, zoo.'

'Did they enjoy it?'

'Charlene hated them peacocks. I had to carry her. My
back was broken by the end of the afternoon.'

The telephone rang.

'Answer that,' she said sharply to me.

It was my agent, on the ball.

'Sal!'

'David, good morning to you.'

'How are things, doll? Feeling better?'

'I'm fine. OK. Yes. Fine.'

'That's my gal. Situation still the same?'

'Mmmmhm.'

'He's gone? Really left you?'

'Yup.'

'I'm sorry. Both of us are really cut up about it. I thought
he . . .'

'It's all right, David. We don't have to go on like this. Tell
me what you were ringing about.'

'I told you on Saturday. They want you to go to New
York. Straight up and down. They'll pay well, an apartment,

all that jazz. Look love, I won't pressure you. I know you must feel like shit, but think about it. It's a very good deal and you could even get an award. You've got to work. Take your mind off things. You've got to think of the future. Hey?'

'I don't ever want to play Pegeen Mike again. I'm sick to death of her. Anything else, David, that can't be impossible. I'd love to play Vladimir.'

'Ha ha!'

'You can laugh.'

'I'll come over.'

I could hear the wheels in his mind turning.

'No.'

'You need a break. Yeah. I recognise that. You've been working too hard and now this . . . Take a couple of weeks off. Go somewhere. I can swing that. The sun. You need some sun. I'll be over on the first plane . . . well, this afternoon sometime. We'll have a great dinner. Guilbaud. Yes. It's all coming to me now. Tomorrow we'll go see them.'

'I want to play Vladimir.'

'We'll fix this whole thing up. You can come back, refreshed, and slip into the last week of rehearsals here, then bingo. Painless, baby. You'll see.'

'Whose side are you on anyway?'

'The Beckett estate wouldn't let you play Vladimir anyway,

so you can put that right out of your mind. Oh, there's been an availability check from Miramax, I'll tell you about that when I see you.'

'I don't want . . .'

'Think of the rest of the cast. Come on baby, just think about it. See you later in the day. Hey, I presume I can stay the night with you?'

He put down the receiver.

I didn't know whether to laugh or cry.

Mrs Murdoch plonked a cup of tea down by the telephone.

'Thanks.'

'I'll make up the spare-room bed. Give the room a little whizz with the Hoover.'

I have never been able to explain to her that telephone calls are private.

'You should pop out and have your hair done. You look like the wreck of the Hesperus.'

'Thanks.'

'No offence meant. You just need someone to give you a little push from time to time.'

She moved towards the door. 'By the way, he'll come back, you know.'

'Mrs Murdoch, how do you know he's gone away?'

She turned her large face towards me and winked. 'There's

not much I don't know in this world. There's not many secrets you can hide from me.'

She and her heavy feet left me, and after a moment I heard her growling voice singing the opening words of an old-fashioned song, 'I Wanna Be Loved By You'.

I picked up the phone and rang the hairdresser.

* * *

I drove home light-headed after my session with the hairdresser. As I got out of the car Jenny stuck her head out of a bedroom window.

'Hey there.'

'Hi.'

'You've had your hair cut.'

'This is the first day of my new life.'

'He was here.'

'Charlie?'

'Un hunh. Mrs Thing wouldn't let him in. She stood at the door with her arms out and said no. She was magic. Like Horatio holding the bridge. I have to get the kids from school, but come in and have a cup of tea when I get back.'

She disappeared, like a jack in the box.

Mrs Murdoch seemed to have picked every flower in the garden and vases round the place were bursting with colour.

I presumed this meant that she approved of what had happened or perhaps she just loved me.

The phone was ringing as I went in the door.

Dear God, I thought, please let it be David saying he has changed his mind.

It was Charlie's mother.

She started right in.

'This is so ridiculous, Sarah. Charlie is so upset. I'm not sure what you think you're doing. He arrived round here the other night in the most awful state. Ronnie and I had gone to bed. It must have been after midnight. It was chaos. For heaven's sake couldn't you have waited until the next day. Lock, stock and barrel. That stuff of his is all over the place and we have people coming to stay next week. I really can't think what we're going to do. He's going to have to find a place very quickly. I mean to say everyone has rows from time to time, but throwing him out is a bit extreme. His father's very upset. He was terribly late going to work this morning. He missed the Dart and had to go in by car. I do think, dear, you should have a little consideration for other people.'

'Hang on.'

'Have you any idea how difficult it is to get a flat these days? Any idea at all. I don't suppose you have. Mary O'Brien had been looking for six months and she just found one the other day and do you know . . .'

'Mona. Mona, let me speak. Mona.'

'What?' she said, her voice angry.

'You don't know what you're talking about. This is between Charlie and myself. You do not have the faintest idea of what goes on between us. He'll get out of your house as soon as he possibly can, just bear with him for a few days, that's all. A week. He'll find himself somewhere in a week. And for your information, he said he was leaving me. I did not throw him out. Get that. He said he was leaving me . . . at, of course, his own convenience. I just said go, now. Now, now. I think you would have done the same.'

'I would never leave Ronnie, no matter what he did. You swear in front of Almighty God to—'

'If you remember, Almighty God took neither part nor parcel in our wedding.' '

'I warned him . . .'

'I'm sure you did. How right you were. You just didn't bring him up very well.'

'How dare—'

'Oh piffle, Mona, don't let's fight about Charlie. I'm just as bad as he is. I'm impossible to live with also. Let's face it, probably everyone in the world is impossible to live with in some way or other. The great thing about me is I'm away quite a lot, so he can do what he wants, though mind you I do draw the line at him fucking other women in my bed.'

'Sarah. How can you say such a dreadful thing . . .'

'Just ask him.'

There was a long silence.

I had had enough. I thought I might be going to cry again.

'I don't believe that Charlie . . . you shouldn't use words like that.'

'Oh, Mona.'

'I am very angry with you, Sarah. Very, very angry. What am I to say to people?'

'Nothing. For heaven's sake. Absolutely nothing. It's no one's business but ours.' I laughed. 'Such a stupid thing to say. I know you'll say what you want. In fact I'm probably the tenth person you've rung today.'

Was I going too far?

I didn't care at that moment.

Clunk.

She had put down the phone.

I stood there for a long time with the receiver in my hand.

Yes, I had gone too far. What on earth was the point in antagonising Mona? On the other hand she has never liked me. She never thought that this actress with no father and whose mother had killed herself was good enough for her lovely son. So piss off Mona.

I put the telephone down.

The house was silent and ever so clean. Mrs Murdoch had really done her ten-euro-an-hour best.

I switched on the TV.

A man in a flak jacket was explaining that there was 'a psychological dynamic at work here.'

Still the sky was heavy with smoke, the rumbling of the passing tanks made my room shake. Bodies lay by the side of the road. Ours or theirs? What the hell did it matter?

My hair was glossy and curling round my face. I could feel the soft curls when I turned my head.

Was I sleeping, while the others suffered? Am I sleeping now?

I honestly don't know.

'Salleee.'

A call across the fence.

'Coming.'

I left the war on, flickering alone in the room, and went next door.

The hall door was open and I could hear the sound of raised voices.

'No. No. No. You may not watch the bloody war.'

'Mu . . . um. I have to.'

'Like hell you have to.'

'Mr Bourke said . . .'

'I don't care – hi Sally, I love the hair – what Mr Bourke says, you may not watch the war. Go and do your homework.'

'This is my homework.'

'I don't believe you. Sit down, Sal. Go, Brendan, now and do your homework. The rest of you, out into the garden.'

'I'm hungry.'

'Look, the lot of you, I'm going to have a quiet cup of tea with Sally, then and not until then, I'll feed you all. Here.' She handed her elder daughter a packet of biscuits. 'Share them. Outside. Now. Brendan, up to your room.'

Having got rid of the children she stared for a moment at me.

'I really do like your hair. I think we'll have a glass of wine. Better than tea any day. Those damn kids, they just want to sit and watch telly. It's like war games to them.'

'I'm watching it too. It's horrible and fascinating. We're all being manipulated.'

'Have you had something done to the colour also?' As she spoke she was getting a bottle of Côtes du Rhône from a cupboard.

'No. Just a really good wash and all that stuff they rub into it. I said everything. Throw everything at it. Ninety euros' worth.'

'Boyo. I hope you feel better.'

She pulled out the cork.

'Temporarily.'

She filled two glasses almost to the brim.

'Sláinte.'

'Hey-o.'

We both drank.

'I don't like them watching the war, but Brendan has this master who seems to think they should. It's history, he says.'

'That's true, and I suppose history mainly entails people killing each other. *Et in saecula saeculorum.*'

'But you say we are all being manipulated.'

'That's part of history too. Just think back to Joan of Arc. Think of the manipulation that went on there. They would have left Tony Blair standing. And poor old Joan got burned.'

'They made her a saint in the end.'

'Fat lot of good that did her, all those hundreds of years later. She was burned. If that happened now your kids could watch it on television. History. We are all history.'

The garden door was flung open and a small girl roared into the room. She threw herself onto her mother's knee.

'They won't let me play.' She buried her face in her mother's shoulder and sobbed.

'See why I needed the wine?' She put her arms round the

child and rocked her gently. 'There. There. Let's give the old face a wipe. That's better. You get a book and sit on the sofa and read it.'

'I don't want to read a book. I want to play with them.'

'And I want to talk to Sally. Ten minutes. On the sofa and then you can help me get the tea. Or you can just sit on my knee and not make a sound. Be like a little mouse.'

'Yes,' said the child.

'Tell me,' I said to Jenny. 'About him coming. What happened?'

'Well, I just heard the car and I looked out of the window and there he was standing on the doorstep with his finger on the bell. Mrs Murdoch took ages to answer.'

'She doesn't think that answering the door is part of her duties.'

'I was about to shout down at him, but she opened the door a crack.' She measured a very small crack with her fingers.

'Mummy,' said the child. 'I don't want you to talk to Sally. I want you to talk to me.' She took hold of her mother's face with her hand and pulled it round to look at her. 'Me.'

'Stop it.' Jenny removed her daughter's fingers and took another slurp of wine. 'I'll put you in the garden and lock the door. Ten bloody minutes is all I want.'

The child started to cry silently. Huge tears rolling down her cheeks.

Her mother ignored her, preferring the silent tears to argument.

'Mrs Murdoch said, "It's you, is it?" and he said, "Yes." And they both stared at each other. "Is she in?" he asked. "She's gone to have her hair fixed," said Mrs Murdoch. More silent staring. "Do you want in?" asked Mrs Murdoch. "Yes please." "Well you can't come in so you might as well be on your way." Then she closed the door and left him standing there.'

I must say I laughed at the picture.

'He rang the bell again and knocked and then finally he kicked the door frame, just down at the bottom right-hand corner, and got into his car and left. He looked pretty cross.'

'Mrs Murdoch is a magic lady.'

'Yep.'

'She worked for Moth for years.'

'Muuuummmy.'

'Sh.'

'I'd better go. I have David arriving.'

'David?'

'Agent. He's going to try and persuade me to go to New York with *Playboy*.'

'Why wouldn't you? You might get an award.'

'That's what he says. I'm so bloody bored with that part,

that production. Everything about it. I want something new to do.'

'I think it would be a godsend. New York. A play you know inside out. Heaven. Away from here.'

'Muuummmy.'

I drained my glass and stood up.

She looked up at me over the head of the little girl.

'Go Sal. Don't be stupid about this. Go.'

'We'll see. Thanks for the wine. Have a good evening. Bye-bye monster.'

The monster glared at me. Her eyes were very blue and guileless.

'Bye,' she said.

* * *

It started to rain again. About six thirty.

No sign yet of David.

Perhaps he had changed his mind, seen the folly of his ways.

Perhaps he was sitting in London Airport experiencing airport rage.

Perhaps he had come round to my way of thinking.

Perhaps . . .

Many perhapses.

It had become almost dark, huge grey clouds pressing down. Just above the roofs.

What fell from the sky was not drops of rain but a sort of greasy mist, unfriendly and very wetting.

I was dressed for Patrick Guilbaud.

I hoped that David would keep his word.

There was a bottle of champagne in the fridge.

Might as well be hanged for a sheep as a lamb.

Moth used to say that a lot. Sort of under her breath, as she was about to have a third glass of something or other, usually gin, or rip open another pack of cigarettes. The poor woman didn't hang around long enough to be killed by either of those pleasures.

I wondered what she would say to me now, if she were still alive.

Some blameful words, I thought.

'I told you this would happen. So often.'

'Aren't you lucky you're not dependent on him?'

'You have to treat men with caution.'

'What the hell did you throw him out for? He'd probably have changed his mind the next morning.'

Those are sort of things she would have said.

She would never have advised me to go and see Grand-father.

She wouldn't have advised me of anything, just pattered out those unhelpful remarks.

I was very tempted to open the bottle of champagne.

I could spend the evening in my best clothes watching the war and drinking champagne; a depressing prospect, but at the moment that thought entered my head I heard the taxi slithering to a stop at the gate.

'What kept you?' I asked as I opened the door.

'I had work to do. I just made the plane by the skin of my teeth. You're looking scrumptious, darling. I must have a great big kiss.'

He dropped his bag on the floor and threw his arms round me. He was a nice man. He could be a pain in the neck from time to time, but in essence he was a nice man. He was a good agent. Just remember that, I said to myself as I stood there in his arms, his warm lips browsing my cheek, getting nearer each second to my mouth.

'Great to see you, David.' I pushed my way out of his grasp. 'Come in, Come in.'

'*Un momento*, darling, just *un momento*. The taxi's waiting. I was afraid we mightn't be able to get one at this time of the evening, so I asked him to wait. Oh my God it's great to see you, doll. It's been too long.'

'Two weeks.'

'Two looong weeks. Get your coat, your bag, all your accoutrements, and let's get underway. By the way I love the hair.'

The champagne could wait.

* * *

The formalities of dining at Guilbaud's were always the same. Hand-kissing, cheek-kissing, glass of champagne, progress to the table, a little wave here or there, maybe a detour to kiss a friend.

David waited until the napkin was tucked across his knee.

'I like this place.'

'Bloody expensive.'

'Worth every penny or cent should I say now?'

He put on glasses to read the menu. I laughed.

'Laugh on,' he said. 'It will happen to you too.'

'Not yet a while anyway. Not in the forseeable future.'

'You can never know. Choose, dear girl. Let's have something terrifically scrumptious.'

We chose, un-chose, re-chose, finally decided.

'That's that.' He grinned at me across the table. 'Now, tell me what the hell's been going on.'

'There's not much to tell. Charlie's left me. I presume that's what you want to know.'

'That I know. I want the whys and wherefores.'

'He's always had the odd affair. This one seems to be serious. Maybe he wanted a wife who was at home most of the time. Maybe he wanted babies. Maybe he just didn't like me any more. Lots of maybes. I haven't dealt with it very well. I'm not much good at writing my own scripts.'

'No one is.'

He took hold of my hand and his thumb rubbed the back of my wrist gently.

'I love him.'

We sat and stared in silence at each other for a long time.

'That's a bit unfortunate,' he said finally. He squeezed my fingers. 'What I mean is it would be much easier if you didn't really care.'

I just shook my head. I was not going to cry in Guilbaud's. Too many people I knew, or who knew me. Anyway I hated crying in public.

He gave my hand a final stroke.

'But I do.' I whispered the words. He had to lean towards me to hear. I got a whiff from him of cigar smoke, wine and very expensive aftershave.

'Baby doll,' he said.

I took my hand away. He could be a pig, sometimes. One day, quite soon, I thought, I would change my agent.

He must have got the drift of my thoughts, because he sat up straight and said in a businesslike voice, 'Let's talk serious talk. Business.'

'Talk away.'

A plate piled with delicious things was put between us.

Our hands rose and fell, our lips munched, he talked as well. I listened.

I knew it all.

I didn't want any part of it. I did not want to go to New York. I didn't care whether I got an award or not. I was sick, sore and tired of Pegeen Mike. I didn't think it would take my mind off things. I wanted to stay at home. But to my surprise I heard my voice agreeing to his suggestions. Yes, I would go in to the theatre tomorrow and we would talk . . . sense. He kept using that word. Finally he picked up my hand and kissed it.

His face was red with wine and bonhomie.

'You're such a star.'

'I'm an idiot more like.'

'I said to Clodagh before I left, the girl has sense. She's just a bit upset, but the sense will out. Wasn't I right?'

'I want to play Vladimir.'

'Ha ha.' He laughed happily and took a slurp of wine. Bastard.

'What about Miramax? Remember? You mentioned them. On the phone.'

'Oh yeah.' He groped in a pocket and brought out a piece of paper. He held it at arm's length and frowned at it.

A sign of approaching age, I thought. The thought made me smile.

'Have you heard of Clara?'

'Clara who?'

'Schumann. You know. Clara Schumann, Schumann's wife.'

'Well, yes of course. Someone just wrote a book . . . who . . . oh God, I forget everything these days . . . Yes, a Scottish writer.'

He peered more closely at the paper. 'Galloway?' he suggested.

'That's it. Janice Galloway. She a terrific writer. Charlie gave me that book for Christmas.'

'Have you read it?'

I shook my head.

I wondered to myself why I hadn't read it.

'They want to talk to you about the part.'

I only read thrillers on tour. Yep. Dozens of thrillers. Good, bad, mediocre.

'Sally.'

'Sorry, David. What did you say?'

'They want to talk to you about the part and as you're going to be in New York . . .'

'What part?'

'If you would concentrate.'

'I am. Totally. I promise.'

'I'm talking work, possible work. I need your attention.

Miramax is talking about Clara. You.' He jabbed a finger at me. 'You. Clara.'

'I wonder where I put the book.'

'I have a script in my case.'

'You should always read the book. At least then you know what the writer is talking about. She was a musician.'

I played a scale on the table with my fingers.

'I will leave it with you. It's very much a first draft.'

'He was mad, wasn't he?'

'Who?'

'Robert. Her husband. Schumann.'

'It's a great part, my darling. Read the script.'

'Yes. Yes, of course. I'll read the book first, if I can find it.'

I put some food onto my fork and put it in my mouth. I chewed for a moment or two.

'Why don't they get Nicole Kidman?'

'They seem to want you. At the moment.'

I rolled my eyes.

'Kidman's too beautiful.'

'Thanks a lot.'

'And maybe she's a tiny bit overexposed these days.'

He picked up my hand and kissed it. His lips were soggy with food and wine.

'Vood I haf to do my Cherman accent.'

He laughed and held my hand tight against his cheek.

'Vy not zee little Zellweger?'

'I don't know why you bother having an agent.'

'So you can get me into the parts I want and out of the parts I don't want. Negotiate, David. Negotiation is the big thing.'

'Yes,' he said, slurping on my hand again. 'We've got some negotiating to do, baby.'

I pulled my hand away from his.

'Just fuck off, David. Think of Clodagh.'

'If it's only Clodagh you're worrying about that's OK. We have a very good arrangement. Believe me, doll. Very, very good.'

He smiled at me, a winey smile. A smile I'd seen before on the faces of lots of men. A good-time smile. A smile that meant so love me baby, for this night I'm all yours. Creep.

I wished I was back watching the war.

'Clodagh and I have a very good arrangement . . .'

Pig.

'You told me.'

'You don't have anything to worry about in that department.'

'I don't. I assure you I don't.'

'Let's have another bottle of wine.'

'I've had enough. I . . .'

'A glass of Sauternes?'

'No thanks.'

'Brandy?'

'I really think . . .'

He made a sweet appealing face at a passing waiter.

'Two brandies please.'

He then gave me a blast of the sweet appealing face.

I laughed.

'You're a dreadful man.'

'A good agent though. You must admit that.'

'A bully.'

'Sometimes necessary.'

'May I just say here and now that I do not want to go to bed with you. You can forget all that stuff.'

'You'll never know what you missed.'

'That's OK by me.'

Amicably we drank several brandies, kissed a lot of people and went home.

* * *

I found it difficult to get to sleep. The room heaved gently and disconcertingly around me; my forehead burst into bubbles of sweat which trickled down my face; my grandfather beckoned me with a long finger and when I tried to get up to go to him he vanished; my mother cried, wailed rather like a wolf that has lost its cub. I was hot, then I was cold, my face was wet with tears and sweat. I tried to read, but the letters on the page wriggled and wormed, I could make nothing of them. I must have finally dropped into sleep because daylight wakened me and I stretched out my arm for Charlie and found emptiness. Filled with hangover and self-pity I turned into my pillow and cried.

* * *

I drank a cup of coffee sitting in front of the TV.

A small child lay in a box, covered with rags. It looked as if it was sleeping; three, four years old, all a life to live ahead of it, the father holding the box, his eyes wild with grief and rage. What can these terrible deaths lead to but rage?

'We are coming with a mighty force to end the reign of your oppressor.'

To kill your children.

To destroy your homes.

To make your lives unbearable.

He should have said those things.

'There is no finer sight to see than twelve thousand American Marines.'

Instead he said that.

'This is rubbish.'

David crossed the room and switched off the set.

'Rubbish. How can you watch it?'

'It's happening.'

'It just could be a mighty spoof. Made for television. Ever thought of that?'

I didn't answer.

'War games. The kids buy them all the time. They're playing war games with us. Grown-up games. Not worth watching, dear heart. For idiots to watch.'

He was eating a banana. He didn't seem to be hung-over at all. My head ached. I knew I looked, as my mother would have said, like the wrath of God. I didn't reply to him. Where was the point?

'Will you drive or shall I call a cab?'

'I'll drive.'

'And then you can take me to the airport?'

'OK.'

'Great. Everything will be settled. Now listen to me, Sally, there's to be no argument. Just smile. Agree with me. Smile, smile but otherwise keep your mouth shut. Understand?'

'Yes. Bully. Smile and smile and be a villain. I expect I can manage that all right.'

'You'll thank me in the end.'

He patted my head as a father might have done.

'You look grim, doll. A little fresh air may perk you up. Let's go, now. Let's drive down to the sea and go into town that way. You can breathe in ozone. Very therapeutic. At this moment what you need is therapy.'

'I've got a bloody, hellish hangover. All your fault.'

'Sea air is the best.'

'I don't understand why you haven't got one too.'

'I'm a man. We have more resistance to alcohol. That's a well-known scientific fact.'

'Oh ha ha.'

'Come on, baby. I feel if I take my eye off you you'll switch on that infernal war machine again. Up, up, up.'

He took hold of my right hand and hauled me to my feet.

He was right about the sea air. Fifteen minutes on Dun Laoghaire pier and I felt better.

A sharp wind blew from the north, across Howth. It stung our faces and tangled my new hair, it brought life back into my brain.

Past the bandstand I stopped walking and stared over the wall towards Howth. I imagined I could see the Bishop's house, in its sheltering grove of trees with the neat lawns and flower bed tilting towards me. I waved, two fingers in the air.

'What's that in aid of?' asked David.

I smiled. 'You know,' I said, instead of answering his question. 'This wonderful harbour is one of the great heritages we got from England. It's so beautiful, don't you think? So solid, staunch. I love it. Kings and queens and armies have all landed here, and all sorts of very important people. It has seen such barbarism and cheers and tears and love and sorrow. People coming, people going, sometimes for ever. Ireland's front door it was for so long.'

He clapped. 'Such eloquence!'

'We just take it for granted. I really do love it. I'd love to have bought a house down here so I could walk the pier every day. So I could keep an eye on it. Make sure no harm came to it.'

'After New York and Miramax you'll be a star, baby. Able to buy a house anywhere in the world.'

'Gee thanks.'

I turned abruptly and began the march back to Dun Laoghaire. Little smacks of wind buffeted my cheeks; there was the smell of rain in the air.

My mother and I had done this walk weekly, usually Sunday afternoons when the pier was crowded with people, dogs, prams. Sometimes, even, a band played in the bandstand and we would stand and listen. This I loved and I resisted her desire to walk on to the lighthouse. The conductor, smart in his army uniform, wore white gloves which flickered and danced around his head as he waved his arms.

'Come on,' she would whisper to me and I would shake my head and keep my eyes fixed on the dancing hands. Finally she would take me by the arm and drag me away.

'That's what I would like to be,' I said once. 'A band conductor.'

'Silly child,' had been her answer.

He took my arm as we walked, just above the elbow, and his fingers kneaded me gently.

He never gives up, I thought, then I thought how mean of me to think such a thing. I giggled; I noticed him smile to himself.

* * *

The meeting was painless.

They all knew they were going to win so their concessions were made with smiling faces.

Yes love, they were so sympathetic.

Yes, they had heard about Charlie, but work was the antidote to sorrow.

Was it not?

Or maybe darling you don't feel sorrow. Relief perhaps?

I just smiled at them. Best not to say a word. David nattered on, negotiating. They smiled at him. A lot of smiling was done. Decent coffee. Now that was remarkable, carried in on a tray by someone's secretary, with real cups and saucers, no plastic mugs, oh boy they wanted me. I had a second cup and the talking went on around me. Three weeks off. I heard that. I wondered if I could find my father in three weeks. I doubted that. They talked money, dates, accommodation, money. I thought about Charlie and the sad faces of the children on the screen. Would I hate New York or love it to death? Their voices rose and fell, they all continued to smile. I drank another cup of coffee. David looked ostentatiously at his watch and scrambled to his feet.

'I have a plane . . .'

I hear him. He put his hand on my shoulder.

'Up, doll. I have a plane . . .'

'Yes. Of course.'

I stood up.

There was a lot of smiling, handshaking, a kiss or two. A sense of relief that it was painlessly over.

'We'll send you the contract,' someone said to David.

'Quickly, quickly. She may change her mind.'

Everyone laughed.

Goodbye.

Three weeks.

Goodbye.

Bon voyage.

We were out in the street, David's hand still on my shoulder, guiding me through the buses and cars, keeping my feet on the ground in case I might fly, escape him. On the pavement he slipped his arm through mine.

'There you are. That wasn't too bad. Was it?'

'I haven't the foggiest idea what you've let me in for.'

'The minimum, darling. I promise you that. Three weeks' hols, starting from today, one week's rehearsal here, another week in the Apple. A nice apartment, West Side, looking on the Park. Three-month run and that's it. No touring. I've left the script by my bed for you to read.'

'We'll see.'

We arrived at the car park.

'Goddammit, baby,' he said. 'I can't have you driving all that way. I'll get a cab.'

'No problem. Really none at all. I'd like to drive you out, I promise you. What's the alternative? Watching the war?'

I put the coins in the machine.

'We won't argue. You're a star.'

It was as always a horrible drive. Stop, start, stop, start. Wait, for what seemed like hours. There were holes in the road, trenches filled with machinery, men resting on spades, cranes, grabs, diggers, traffic lights, diversions, but in the end we made it.

'Next time you come,' I said, 'it won't be so bad.'

He kissed me and grabbed his bag from the back seat.

'Now listen here to me, you're not to go changing your mind about all this. I've got you a great deal.'

I patted his cheek. 'You don't have to worry. I'll be as good as gold. You find me another movie though. I'd like a good movie. The Coen brothers. I'd like to work for them.'

'So would every other actor in the world.'

'You're my agent. Fight for me.'

I drove off, leaving him standing there with his hand in the air.

I didn't drive straight back into town, I went cross-country towards Malahide and then veered off to Howth.

There was a man cutting the grass; he paid no attention to my arrival.

I rang the bell and waited.

No sound.

I rang again.

After a minute or two the lawnmower stopped. I turned and looked towards the lawn. The man was approaching me.

'Yes?' he shouted in my direction.

I waited until he got close to me.

'Is there no one in?'

'I'd say he'd be in there. He's not one for going out at all.

It's her day off. Tuesday's always her day off. I'm here Tuesday. Odd jobs, I do.' He gestured towards the lawn-mower. 'I come on Thursdays too, but she's here on Thursdays. She gives me a bite of lunch. Mind you, she leaves me something on Tuesday. You have to have a bite to eat. She leaves something for him too. Pie it was today. I put it in the microwave. They have a microwave. A very handy gadget.'

'Could you let me in?'

'Ah well now . . .'

'I'm his granddaughter.'

He looked at me with a certain surprise.

'I never heard tell . . .'

'Well I am. I'd like to see him.'

'No one told me . . . I don't think I can let you in. They always tell me if . . .'

'You could go and ask him.'

'I suppose I could.'

But he didn't move.

We both stood quite still, staring at each other, and suddenly I heard the door behind me creak open. I turned and saw the Bishop standing in the doorway. He was wearing a long silk dressing gown; his face was gaunt, but deep in his eyes were sparks.

We all spoke at the same time.

'Grandfather . . .'

'What, may I ask, is going on?'

'She says she's your granddaughter.'

'That's correct. She is what she says she is.'

'I didn't know what to . . .'

'You have done very well, thank you, Corcoran. That will be all.'

Corcoran bowed deeply.

A laugh came up in my throat.

'And you,' he said coldly. 'I suppose you want to come in.'

I nodded and moved past him through the door.

He closed the door behind us.

The hall was dim and warm, smelling of furniture polish. The only light came from a tall window halfway up the stairs, it lay like tissue paper across the hall floor.

I took a deep breath. 'Would you mind if I were to make myself a cup of tea . . . and you too if you'd like one?'

'I will do it. Please wait in the drawing room. Mrs Carruthers does not like strangers in her kitchen.'

I wondered how often she had had strangers in her kitchen.

'It's all right, Grandfather. Don't bother. I won't die without a cup of tea.'

'I will make you one. I am perfectly capable of boiling a kettle. Please go in to the drawing room.' I went in and I heard his feet stepping with confidence along the passage to the kitchen.

A fire crackled in the grate. There were flowers on the tables and cupboards, charming spring flowers, bright red rhododendrons, and pale azaleas heaped in a shallow dish. He had been sitting by the fire in his high-backed chair and a pile of papers lay on the floor beside it. The mower had started up again in the garden, and I stood by the window and watched Corcoran as he walked backwards and forwards across the grass guiding the machine. I wondered if they knew about the war. This place seemed so old-fashioned, so out of life. I wondered if he would leave the place to me.

Pretty unlikely.

Who else had he to leave it to?

Mrs Carruthers?

She probably deserved it.

I thought of myself driving out here each evening after the show, letting myself in to this pristine palace. No Charlie, no neighbours, no children or cats. I didn't like the thought.

I could sell it and move to Dalkey, home of the stars. I could bring with me those ghostly portraits and invent histories for them. I could have them as my family.

I heard a step and turned. He came slowly into the room carrying a tray. It looked too heavy for his thin arms to bear. I crossed the room and took it from him.

'I had to drive my agent to the airport so I thought I might as well come and say hello.'

I put the tray on a table near the fire.

'Scones too. How lovely.'

'Mrs Carruthers seems to think that maybe I will die of hunger when she goes out. I don't normally have visitors, but she behaves as if I have them every day. She leaves everything just so for me, trays set, table laid. I have nothing to do, only eat.'

'How lucky you are.'

'Some people might think so.'

He sat down in his chair. He laid his head against the back of the chair and closed his eyes.

'Pour,' he said. His voice sounded tired. I did as I was told and placed his cup on a small table near to his hand.

'So, this man, I presume he's a man, this agent. What was he doing here?'

I poured myself some tea and took a scone.

'Persuading me to take a job I didn't want. Then negotiating. I'm hopeless at negotiating. Usually I want the job so badly that I don't care what they pay me. Managements know that. They just take one look at me and say here's a sucker.' I sat down opposite to him. I balanced my cup and saucer on the arm of the chair and took a bite from the scone.

'What about this job you don't want to do?'

'It's a lovely part and I'm good in it, but I've been hawking it round Europe for so long I'm sick to death of it, and now I go and tie myself up for another few months. Bloody New York.'

A slight smile flickered on his mouth. 'I've never been to New York,' he said.

'*Playboy.*'

'Ah yes. I saw you in that also.'

There was quite a long silence.

'They hope we'll get awards.'

He nodded. 'You were good.'

'Do you go a lot to the theatre?'

'When I have a specific interest. I'm afraid the standard here has become very low. I go seldom now. *Playboy* was the last thing I saw. Mrs Carruthers drives me in in the car and then picks me up afterwards. She meets a friend, has a coffee. I don't think it troubles her too much. She is a very fine woman.'

'I'm sure she is.'

'Yes.'

We became silent once more. I thought about him sitting alone in the theatre.

'Maybe sometime you might come with me?'

'Come with you?'

'To the theatre.'

'Ah.'

'If there was something on that was really good, we might go together. I could pick you up and bring you home. Save Mrs . . .'

'I think not. Thank you.'

'As you wish.'

The scone was delicious.

He stared at me dolefully and then drank some tea. He searched for a handkerchief and patted his mouth. He longed for me to be gone.

'You weren't as good as Siobhan McKenna. She was the best Pegeen I have ever seen. A bit old but . . . You ran her close. I have a great attachment to that play.'

'But you can see, can't you, how you could get tired of the whole thing. Night after night. On and on. I almost hate it now. I'm so afraid that my hate will show through in my performance. The relief I felt that last night. "*Oh my grief, I've lost him surely. I've lost the only playboy of the western world.*" And inside I was hectic with joy. Never, never again. Yippee. Anyway now I have three weeks' holiday then I plunge back in. Maybe I'll feel better about it by then. What do you think?'

He leaned back in the chair and closed his eyes. Outside the lawnmower purred. I gulped my tea and got up.

'I'm going, Grandfather'

He didn't answer.

'Will I bring the tray back into the kitchen?'

He didn't answer.

'Well bugger you,' I said very softly.

I left the room.

I waved to Corcoran as I got into the car, but he paid no attention.

* * *

The war intensified. The black clouds seemed to fill my sitting room, seep under closed doors. I woke each morning to the smell of smoke, burning metal, cooking flesh. I hated turning on my television and yet I couldn't leave it alone.

'Opposition is futile. Defeat is inevitable,' Nick Witchell told us. His face was pursed and gloomy as he spoke the words. John Simpson was wounded by friendly fire. Dazed, he carried on reporting, blood running down the side of his face. We watched it over and over again. Take him home, I wanted to shout, take him home and put him to bed. Give him black coffee and lots of TLC. The man has to be in a state of shock. Pipelines burned, sad mothers screamed for their injured children. Does anyone understand what the hell is going on? Even when I turned off the set I could hear their cries in my ears.

I started to read *Clara*. Yes, I thought. This could be my part. Yes. He's right. Kidman is too beautiful. I flipped some other stars through my head. I would have to look at the script. Yes. It would be so easy to screw this one up . . . but looking at the novel, this could well be my part.

I read *Godot* again.

I wondered if that crosspatch old man, that Bishop, had ever seen it. I then wondered if he watched the war. No. He didn't know about it. I bet the TV was in the kitchen for the delectation of Mrs Carruthers, who would look at *Neighbours, EastEnders, Coronation Street* and the European Song Contest. Maybe old Doris Day movies; certainly not the war.

Charlie rang twice; each time I heard his voice I put down the receiver.

Each time I did that, I regretted doing it.

His mother phoned me again.

'Charlie wants to see you,' she said in a peremptory voice as soon as I had picked up the receiver.

'I don't want to see him. I've told you that. I've told him that. How many people do I have to tell?'

'No need to be so cross, my dear.'

'Why not? Answer me that. Why the hell should I not be cross?'

She sighed. 'I am trying very hard to do the right thing,'

she said. 'I am not a person who is renowned for my tact.'

'Mona . . .'

'I think you may be having a little breakdown. You should get help.'

'Thank you.'

'No need for sarcasm.'

Someone spoke to her at her end of the phone.

'He's here now. Will you . . .'

I put the phone down. I switched on the TV fortissimo; guns and smoke pounded into the room. I was crying.

*   *   *

I think I must have spent three days in such a fuzz of almost madness. I didn't dress, I didn't answer the doorbell or the telephone, I didn't open my post. I let it pile on the floor under the letter box. My head throbbed and I felt constantly hungry. I read and reread *Godot*. I paced the floor, downstairs and upstairs.

> *A dog came in the kitchen*
> *And stole a crust of bread*
> *Then cook up with a ladle*
> *And beat him till he was dead.*

Then all the dogs came running
And dug the dog a tomb,
And wrote upon the tombstone
For the eyes of dogs to come:

A dog came in the kitchen
And stole a crust of bread
Then cook up with . . .

On and on. The rhythm of the words made a barrier in my mind: too high for thoughts to scramble over, too high for tears to spill.

Then cook up with a ladle

Mrs Murdoch came and went.

She paid little attention to me; she sang tunelessly or whistled as she pushed the Hoover across the carpets.

And beat him till he was dead.

She put my clothes in the washing machine and then took them out to the line in the garden and cracking each garment in turn she pegged them on the line.

She brought me cups of coffee and tucked the blanket

round me as I crouched on the sofa.

'That Bush should be taken out and shot,' was one of her few remarks.

Another, just before she left.

'There's no need for you to be getting like your mother.'

I answered neither remark. But the second one went into whatever remained of my brain.

Then all the dogs came running

She left me snacks to eat and put flowers in the vases.

On day five I turned off the television at half past eleven in the morning. I listened to the silence.

It was more comfortable than the war.

The telephone rang and I answered it.

It was Mrs Carruthers. 'Good morning, miss.'

'Good morning, Mrs Carruthers. Is everything all right?'

'The Bishop would like you to take him for a drive, miss.'

'Oh . . . ah, yes. When?'

'It is a lovely day for a drive. A lovely day.'

I looked out of the window and saw to my surprise that it was a lovely day indeed. 'Yes,' I said. 'That would be good. I'd like a drive too.'

'I'll drop him over to you so. In about three-quarters of

an hour. You can leave him back here in the afternoon sometime.'

She put down the receiver.

I flew upstairs to the bathroom.

> And wrote upon the tombstone
> For the eyes of dogs to come:
> A dog came in the kitchen

He walked up the path to the hall door like a soldier, back straight, legs swinging in good order; Mrs Carruthers pattered behind him with a grey shawl over one arm and a walking stick in her other hand. I watched them from the study window.

He rang the bell. I opened the door and went to embrace him, but he shifted, so I embraced the air beside him. He smiled sourly.

'What a good idea this is.'

He moved past me into the hall and stood there staring round.

Mrs Carruthers handed me the shawl and the walking stick. 'Just in case,' she said.

'Thank you. Won't you come in and have a cup of coffee?'

She shook her head. 'Don't delay,' she whispered and turning she walked briskly back to her car.

'Would you like a cup of coffee, Grandfather?'

'No, I would not. When I want to go for a drive, I mean a drive. I can have coffee at home.'

'All right. Let's go.'

Luckily my bag and keys were on the hall table so I didn't have to delay him any longer.

I helped him into the car.

I held the shawl out towards him; angrily he gestured it away. I threw it and the stick onto the back seat.

'She fusses so,' he said.

'Where would you like to go? Fasten your seat belt. Or would you like me to do it for you?'

'I can manage perfectly well.'

He struggled with his belt.

'I would like to have lunch in Hunter's Hotel and then perhaps we might walk for a while in the garden . . . that garden . . . you know, Walpole's garden.'

'Walpole is dead.'

'You know where I mean.'

'Yes.'

'All right' he said.

He didn't speak again until we reached the Glen of the Downs, but his eyes took in everything we passed, each change, each tree that had been cut, each widening of the road, each housing estate. As we passed the hotel he sighed.

'I used to take your mother there when she was a child. For lunch. Saturday lunch. And her mother. There was a nice lunch on Saturday and Sunday, but of course I had other things to do on Sunday.'

'I don't think you would like it now.'

'I don't suppose so. I think your mother used to enjoy it. There were always other children there. She would run around with them. She was a pretty child.'

I noticed his eyes were on my face.

'I've seen pictures of her. Yes, she was pretty. She was always pretty distracted-looking a lot of the time, but . . .'

'It doesn't matter.'

'What doesn't matter?'

'Nothing matters. When you get to my age, nothing matters. It is important to remember that.'

He lapsed once more into silence.

At the turn off to Delgany he sighed again. 'Delgany,' he said.

'Would you like to go and look?'

'No. Nothing is any longer as I remember it to be. This can be painful.'

'I don't think Delgany has changed all that much.'

'My grandfather was Rector there.'

'Well that can't have been today or yesterday.'

'A long time, certainly. Yes. As a small child I used to visit them. Stay actually, sometimes for a week or two. They had an orchard with cherry trees. My governess and I used to go in the pony trap to Greystones on sunny days. If it were warm enough I would be allowed to swim.'

'I bet that wasn't very often. The sea in Greystones is colder than anywhere else in the world.'

He smiled.

That surprised me; I couldn't remember ever having seen him smile before; for a moment or two his face became soft, and he looked very like Moth.

'I didn't know your grandfather was a clergyman.'

'Army, navy, Church,' he said somewhat inexplicably. Then after a few moments, 'It was a way of life. Laid out, planned. You took what was coming to you.'

Silence.

His face hardened once more.

I wondered had I a right to question him further; I decided that I had not.

Hunter's Hotel stood, calm, almost eternal in its bend of the road. Across from it behind a wall the trees were starting to burst, green leaves unfolding. I drove into the yard and helped the Bishop out of the car. I handed him the stick; scornfully he waved it away.

'I am not a cripple.'

In the dark hallway an elderly woman was waiting. She

shook his hand warmly. 'Bishop, it's been too long. We were so pleased when Mrs Carruthers rang this morning. We always have room for old friends.'

She turned to me and shook my hand. 'You're the granddaughter? Everyone who has seen your Pegeen says it was wonderful. Congratulations. Is she a star, Bishop?'

'What's a star? Hunh? Glitter.' He turned abruptly and went into the bar. 'Two dry sherries. That's what we'll have and the menu. If you please.'

She patted my shoulder and then pushed me gently after him.

He sat himself down by the window in a chair with a loose floral cover. Behind him in the garden daffodils rippled in the wind.

'Glitter. Do you consider yourself to be a star?'

I laughed.

'That's no answer.'

'I haven't given it a thought. I'd like to be very good at my job. That wouldn't make me a star though, that's all to do with personality. People shouldn't notice you when you're off the stage. But you notice stars. You have to notice stars.'

The elderly lady appeared with two glasses of sherry on a silver tray. She put a glass in front of each of us.

'Just a token,' she said. 'To show how glad we are, Bishop,

to see you back. After a long time. Such a long time. Too long.'

She laid the menu on the table between us and smiled.

'Thank you.' He bowed slightly towards her as he spoke.

'Thank you,' I muttered.

'My wife died, you know. I haven't been out too much since . . .'

'Yes. I heard that sad news.'

'. . . that occurrence.'

'I do understand. May I recommend the roast beef. It is very good today, cooked to perfection.'

'Yes. We'll both have that. Pink. We like it pink.'

'Of course. A little soup to start with or perhaps some pâté de campagne?'

'What's the soup?'

'Carrot and orange and of course there's a fine consommé, if you preferred that.'

'We'll have carrot and orange.'

'Thank you. Your table's the end one on the right, looking out at the garden. Come in whenever you've finished your sherry.'

She picked the menu up and left.

'Talk about customer manipulation. Anyway, who told you that I liked my roast beef pink?'

He smiled sheepishly. 'I presumed.'

'I noticed.'

He raised his glass towards me. 'Here's to . . .'

'To what?'

'I don't know.'

'Family life,' I said.

He drank down half the glass in one go. 'Good sherry,' he said.

'Family life,' I said.

What a hope, I thought as I said it.

When we went in to lunch he ordered a bottle of St Emilion.

'I can only drink a small glass,' I said. 'I'm driving.'

'Clerics are famous for their consumption of fine wine.' He smiled again briefly. 'Some clerics, that is. Alas, poverty prevents others from indulging.'

'You were one of the lucky ones.'

He looked out of the window across the garden to where a little stream ran. He said nothing.

We spoke little during the meal.

He ate as if Mrs Carruthers had not fed him for days. He poured me a small glass of wine and then topped up his own glass until the bottle was empty.

He had difficulty in standing up.

'I'll go and get your stick,' I said.

'No. I can use you as a stick.' He hauled himself from his

chair and leant on my shoulder. He was all bones, but we managed to walk with a certain dignity to the door. Old ladies turned and stared after us. The owner came out from the office and pattered after us along the hall.

'Bishop.'

We stopped at the front door.

He turned towards her and waited for her to speak.

'Was your lunch all right?'

'Very excellent. Thank you. Excellent. Yes,' he said.

'Wonderful,' I said.

'I do hope you'll come again. We like old friends to come.'

'I am in the hands of my granddaughter these days.'

'Yes,' I said. 'We'll come again. Definitely.'

'Old age, you know . . . but it's not too far for Sally to drive me. From time to time. Yes. From time to time,' He held out his hand and she shook it.

'You will always be very welcome, Bishop.'

She stood smiling by the door until we had turned the corner.

I helped him into the car and fastened his seat belt. His head hung down towards his chest, his eyes were shut.

So we travelled back to Howth. As we turned in his gateway, his eyes opened. 'Home,' he said.

Mrs Carruthers must have been watching from the window

because she had the door open by the time we arrived and was standing waiting to help him from the car. Magisterially he waved her away, and levered himself out without any help. He strode to the front door and then turned, his hand in the air as if he were sending her a blessing.

'Mrs Carruthers will drive me to your house next Saturday and we will do the same thing.'

He was gone before I could reply. Mrs Carruthers took his stick and the rug from the back seat.

'Thank you,' she murmured. 'I know he means to say thank you.'

'That's OK. He's had quite a lot to drink. I couldn't . . .'

'We pass no remarks.'

She shut the door and followed him into the house.

* * *

Jenny's children were all in my garden when I got home, and half the fence was lying on the ground.

I unlocked the glass door and went out.

'Well, well. What have we here?'

'It's all right,' said Brendan. 'Dad will fix it.'

'What happened?'

'We were playing football and . . .'

'It wasn't our fault. We told Derry not to go over the fence and . . .'

'Who is Derry?'

'You know Derry. He's in forty-two.'

'Where is Derry?'

'Your fence was very wobbly.'

'Shut up, ninnycompoop.'

'It was so, wobbly.'

'He's gone home.'

'Mummy sent him home. Go on home to your own bloody house, she said.'

'Bloody, bloody, bloody.'

'So Derry climbed on it and it fell over?'

There was a long pause.

'More or less,' said Brendan cautiously. The others were watching him. 'I went too.'

'Bloody, bloody.'

'And then ... we all went and it fell.'

'Hannah cut her knee.'

'It really wasn't our fault.'

'Show Sally your knee, Hannah.'

Hannah obligingly pulled down her jeans and showed me a large piece of sticking plaster on her knee.

'I tore my trousers.'

'Poor you,' I said.

'Mummy says she'll have to throw them out.'

'Bloody, bloody, bloody.'

Jenny's head appeared over the bit of fence that was still standing.

'Oh God, Sally. I'm so sorry.'

'It wasn't your fault.'

'The little bastards . . . Don will fix it up. I've given out to them all and I sent bloody Derry home.'

'Bloody, bloody, bloody.'

'He'll be home soon. He's at the Leinster match. He'll . . . over the weekend. He'll . . .'

'Let's just forget it.'

'If,' said Brendan helpfully, 'we just cleared all this stuff away, we could leave it open. Then . . .'

'No,' said his mother. 'Don't even think such a thing. Come and have a glass of wine, Sal.'

'I think it's a great idea. Then we could just run in and . . .'

'Shut up, Brendan. Sally must have a little protection from the lot of you. Wine, Sal?'

'Yes. I think I need one.'

I picked my way carefully through the debris. One clematis gone, three rose bushes, gone, one nice yellow azalea which had been flowering when I left the house that morning, gone, and a lot of weeds, gone.

Jenny took my arm and pulled me towards the house.

'We'll replace the plants.'

'I . . .'

'Of course we will. God, they're such brats. I hate them, hate them all. Red or white?'

'Red.'

The bottle was on the table and already open; Jenny's half-empty glass stood beside it.

'Help yourself.'

I filled my glass to the brim.

'I honestly thought someone was dead. Well, just for a moment. The crash and then Hannah screaming, then they all yelled for me. There are times I wish . . . I was like you . . . no fucking kids.'

'No fucking husband either.'

Jenny laughed.

Then we both laughed.

There was an amazing silence in the garden.

We touched glasses.

'What do you think they're up to.'

'I don't give a damn.'

We sat down in two wicker chairs that crackled as they took our weight; we turned them with their backs to the window.

Jenny sighed with relief. 'I hate drinking on my own, so your arrival was most opportune. Where have you been? We saw you go off with Beelzebub this morning. I thought you might never return.'

'My grandfather Beelzebub.'

'That was the man himself? The Bishop?'

'The very man.'

'Oh my God. I should have had a better look. Where did you go?'

'Hunter's. For lunch. It wasn't too bad. He hardly spoke. I hardly spoke. We had a good lunch and I delivered him home in one piece. He wants to do it again next Saturday.'

'And on and on for ever?'

'We can't do that. I have to go to New York.'

'You've made your mind up?'

'Yup. Well, it was made up for me. I feel a bit grim about it, but I guess it must be the right thing to do. Maybe you might dump the kids and come out for a few days?'

'What a wonderful thought. I've never been to New York. Do you really mean that?'

'It would be great if you could. Don't come for the first night, that'll be hell, but any time after that. I'll be free every day. Here's to New York.' I raised my glass.

She raised hers. 'I wonder. I wonder.'

'Jump,' I said.

We both started to laugh again.

Don came in and found us still laughing.

'Two pissed ladies in my kitchen and the garden on fire,' he said.

'What?'

We suddenly became aware of smoke curling into the kitchen. He ran out and we followed him, clutching our glasses. About twelve children were standing round a bonfire, the flames of which snapped and crackled jovially and leapt high into the evening sky. It had been neatly built where the fence had been, where my roses and azalea had been. Smoke curled into the kitchen.

'Brendan.' Jenny let a yell out of her.

Smoke curled into my eyes and throat.

'We're just clearing up,' Brendan shouted from the other side of the bonfire. He threw what looked horribly like my azalea onto the fire and a fountain of sparks sprayed upwards.

'Would someone tell me what is going on?'

More smoke curled into my eyes and throat. I wanted to cough. I took a drink from my glass.

'Jenny, would you tell me what is going on?'

'Pour yourself a glass of wine.'

She came back into the kitchen and closed the door. 'I suppose they might as well get on with it now they've got that far.' She sat down and started to laugh. 'We were never allowed to do such crazy things. Will they grow up better adjusted than we did? Will they be full of confidence? Will they love the world? Will they love their parents?'

'They'll probably be psychopathic fire-raisers.'

'How was the match?'

'We lost.'

'Oh darling.' She took his hand and kissed it. 'What a shame.'

He held onto her hand and kissed it. 'It's so nice to come home to a quiet, well-organised home. Everything calm and dinner on the table.'

'Oh God, dinner!' said Jenny.

I thought it best to go, so I drained my glass and slipped out and went back to my own calm and peaceful home.

The phone was ringing.

I didn't want to answer it.

It might be Charlie's mother.

It might be David.

It might be Mrs Carruthers to say that the Bishop was dead.

It might be any one of many loving, caring friends.

It might be the ghost of Moth . . . that thought twitched a smile onto my face, made me stretch out my hand and pick up the receiver.

It was, of course, Charlie.

'Look here . . .' he began.

The only thing to do at such a moment is to put the receiver down.

I didn't.

'Fuck off, Charlie,' I said instead.

'Are you all right?'

'Why wouldn't I be? How's Marianna?'

'Nobody's seen you. I was worried.'

'I am not Moth. I wouldn't ever do what she did.'

'Can I come round?'

'I'm sure you can.'

'May I? You know what I mean. May I, Sal? Please.'

Then I put down the receiver and stood, my heart beating like a drum inside my ribs. I held onto the wall. The phone rang

and rang

and rang

and then stopped and the silence was an unforgiving silence.

I switched on the television and sat in the gathering dark watching the world making a fool of itself, and outside in the garden the children danced around the flickering remains of my fence and my azalea.

* * *

Sunday bells no longer seem either as loud or as urgent as they used to be. Nowadays they are almost apologetic. Please, they say, please. I lay in bed and thought about

Grandfather and the sound of the bells rolled round in my head and there was still the smell of last night's bonfire drifting in the air. What had he been like as a young man, I wondered. Handsome? That was obvious. Full of religious zeal? Probably. He had the autocratic air of a zealot. But there was an anger locked inside him that surely should be foreign to a bishop. In my mind bishops should be full of love and goodwill towards men; neither of these attributes could I seem to find in Grandfather. Maybe I wasn't looking hard enough. I was merely going on the impressions he was giving me.

Prospero. I heard his mellifluous voice saying those words.

> '. . . now I want
> Spirits to enforce, art to enchant;
> And my ending is despair
> Unless I be relieved by prayer,
> Which pierces so that it assaults
> Mercy itself, and frees all faults.
> As you from crime would pardoned be,
> Let your indulgence set me free.'

I wondered if he went to church any more, under the watchful eye of Mrs Carruthers, or did he send her to pray for him, while he sat by the fire and wrote his past in his notebooks. I couldn't pray for him, that was sure. To whom could I possibly pray?

Moth had seen to that all right.

I remember coming home from school one day filled with the enthusiasm of an eight-year-old for the newly learnt thing. I ran into the kitchen where she had been making bread.

'I have a father,' I had shouted to her. She turned from the oven and stared at me. Her hair was dishevelled and she had flour on her hands and arms.

'What?'

'Miss Murphy said.'

'What does Miss Murphy know about it?'

'Our Father which art in heaven . . .'

She slammed her hands down on the table.

'Stop that.'

'Why? I . . .'

'There is no father in heaven. There is no heaven. Stories. All stories. There is no God to pray to. No comfort. There is nothing, only the world and people. Bad people, good people, middling people. There is nothing else. No bloody thing else.' She took a deep breath. 'Now, go and do your homework.'

That was her clear and unequivocal belief. I didn't fight against it, and gradually I began to believe it too; not I have to say with the anger and passion that she had, but nonetheless I believed her to be right. I have never been troubled by my beliefs/non-beliefs, whichever you prefer to call them, but I would now, at this moment, like to have someone to pray to on behalf of my grandfather.

It was luxurious to lie in bed, propped by pillows, books scattered on the blankets, *Godot*, *Playboy* and a thriller set in Venice by Donna Leon. I only wished my thoughts a little less lugubrious. I hadn't yet looked out of my window so I had no idea what sort of a mess I would find out there when I finally got up. Yawning and stretching and dozing and dipping in and out of Donna Leon were my plans for the immediate future.

Bells, scraping, whispers, and the steady creaking of an unoiled wheel, the odd giggle and weaving through such sounds the memory of his voice.

> *And my ending is despair*
> *Unless I be relieved by prayer,*

I wondered, again, if he went to church.

Probably; driven by Mrs Carruthers, both of them sitting bolt upright in the car. She would be wearing a hat, I felt sure, and would smile and duck her head at the parishioners as they passed. He would ignore them.

Which pierces so that it assaults
Mercy itself, and frees all faults.

Does he know about mercy?

I doubt that.

I wish I had known him through all my years.

I wish I had climbed on his knees and pulled his hair, had whispered mighty secrets into his ear. It is too late to start that sort of thing now.

Yes.

I was drifting into sleep again. Whispers, a cough, giggles, scrape, a door opened very, very quietly, bells, Grandfather's voice crying in the wilderness prepare ye the way of the Lord, make straight in the desert a highway for our God. Clink and the sound of a tap, mercy, despair, gentle footsteps. My eyes flickered open, shut. The day was grey beyond the window. Wishfully, I smelt coffee. Wishfully. My eyes opened. Coffee. I do smell coffee. Bugger! Who the hell is making coffee?

I got out of bed and flew down the stairs.

Charlie was sitting at the table in the kitchen, reading the Sunday *Indo*, as if he owned the place, coffee steaming in a mug beside him.

'Charlie!'

'I wondered how long it would be.' He waved a hand towards the cooker. 'Coffee?'

'What are you doing here? How did you get in?'

He raised his eyebrows and looked towards the window. Outside Don was sitting on a pile of stones, with a mug of coffee on the grass beside him. He raised a hand in my direction. Around him his children were clearing ashes away.

'My fault,' he called out to me. 'Sorree.'

'Fink.'

He grinned cheerfully at me.

I went over to the cooker and poured myself a cup of coffee. One thing I had to say about Charlie was that he made a good cup of coffee. I brought it to the table and sat down.

'What do you want?' I asked him.

He folded the paper and tucked it into the back of his chair.

'Are you all right?'

'What do you want?'

He picked up his mug and stared at me through the rising steam.

I leant towards him. 'What do you want?'

'People said they hadn't seen you.'

'You spoke to me on the telephone yesterday. You knew . . .'

'Nothing. Alive. I knew you were alive. That was all.'

'That's all you need to know. Would you go now?'

He waved his coffee cup at me. 'I'll just have another cup of coffee.' He got up and went over to the stove. 'I had to throw my shoes out.'

'Good.'

'They cost me two hundred euro.'

'So?'

He poured some coffee. He put four sugar lumps in the mug and swirled them with a spoon.

'Your teeth will rot in your head.'

'That's not your business any longer.'

He threw in another lump.

I said nothing.

'Where were you?' he asked.

'That's not your business either. I was here. Watching the war. Feeling bloody awful if you really want to know.'

'Watching the war!' His voice was filled with scorn.

'It's history. I admit it's only the acceptable face of death and destruction. They show us what they think we can bear. I think we have a duty to watch it. It's happening, for God's sake. The world will never be the same again.'

I felt tears coming into my eyes and leant forward, my head on my hand so that he wouldn't see.

'That's your point of view.'

'Yes.'

'It certainly isn't mine.'

'It wouldn't be.'

'Sally.'

'Mmmm?'

'I think we're both being foolish . . .' His mobile played its silly tune. He groped in his pocket for it. He stared at the number.

'Excuse me.'

He walked quickly across the room and out into the hall, holding the phone in front of him as if it might explode at any moment. He closed the door behind him.

'I told you not to . . .' His voice descended into a whisper.

I wondered whether to press my ear to the door, but decided not to. I looked out into the garden; Don was scooping twigs and small bits of fence up into the barrow; the children had disappeared. Charlie's voice murmured behind me in the hall. I cleared my throat. I began to sing.

> *A dog came in the kitchen*
> *And stole a crust of bread*
> *Then cook up with a ladle*
> *And beat him till he was dead.*
>
> *Then all the dogs came running*
> *And dug the dog a tomb,*

And wrote upon the tombstone
For the eyes of dogs to come:'

Don straightened up and looked at me. He threw his head
back.

'Owowowow.'

A rat came into my garden

'Owowow.'

With another rat in tow.

'Owowowow.'

Charlie came back into the room tucking his mobile into
his pocket. 'I have to go,' he said.

'No one's stopping you.'

Good repartee that, I thought.

'Look, Sal . . .'

'Go. Marianna calls. Just fucking go.'

'No need to get ratty.'

'Every need. Go on, out or I'll throw another cup of
coffee at you.'

I moved towards him in what I hoped was a menacing
way. He backed towards the door.

'They tell me you're not going to America.'

'They tell you wrong. But you're not to think you
can come sneaking back in here when I'm out of the
country.'

'I'd never . . .'

'Out.'

We were in the narrow hall. He put out a hand and took hold of a banister.

'You're menacing me,' he said.

'Yes.'

'I'd like to come back again. I need to talk to you. Sally. This is my home.'

'My home.'

'Our home. I want to . . .'

'No.' I pushed past him and opened the hall door. 'Out. Now.'

He raised his hands in a despairing gesture and walked out through the door. He turned to speak and I shut the door in his face. He looked dejected. I felt very dejected. I felt so dejected that I couldn't even bear to turn on the war. I wished I hadn't seen him. I wished I had listened to whatever it was he had to say. I wished he hadn't gone so easily. I wished he hadn't come. I wished a whole jumble of contradicting wishes. I wished that Moth wasn't dead. I wished that I had a father. I wished that I didn't have to do *Playboy*. I wished, I wished, I wished.

That was Sunday finished with.

* * *

Monday.

Tuesday.

Wednesday I was woken by the telephone.

It was Mrs Carruthers.

'He would like to see you at eleven o'clock.'

No good morning, how are you today or any other niceties.

'Is he ill?'

'No. He just wants to see you. Will that be all right?'

'I'm still in bed.'

Silent disapproval made its way down the line.

'All right. Yes. I'll be there. Elevenish.'

'Thank you, miss. There will be coffee waiting.'

I could hear Mrs Murdoch hoovering downstairs. A normal, everyday sound, hoovering, soothing, as long as someone else is using the machine. Someone like Mrs Murdoch. She looked at me as I came into the room. She switched off the machine.

'You're more yourself,' she said. 'There were a couple of days there I thought you were losing it. What happened the garden? Want a cuppatea?'

'No thanks. I have to go out. I have to go and see the Bishop.'

She raised her eyebrows. 'My my.'

'The garden.'

I walked over to the window and looked out. It didn't look good. Most of the fence was down and my flower bed looked like a battlefield; there was a heap of ash where the bonfire had been.

'The kids next door knocked down the fence, trampled my plants to death and then Don came and cleared the whole thing up, knocked down some more fence and had a bonfire.'

'Did you give them a good clattering?'

'No. I'm not the clattering type.'

She sniffed and trod heavily to the stove. She lit the gas under the kettle.

'Well if you're not having a cup, I am, and a cigarette. I like a cigarette at this time of the morning.'

She always said this; I think it was to indicate to me that she was not a chain smoker, just puffed the odd time during the day.

'They need a good clatter, destroying other people's property like that.'

'I think it was an accident.'

She sniffed. 'Accident!' she said. She took a pack of cigarettes from the pocket of her overall and put it on the table and then her lighter balanced beside it. 'What are you going see that ould bastard for?'

'The Bishop? Rough words, Mrs M.'

'Your poor mother hated him. God rest her. Hated him.' She threw a tea bag into a mug angrily. 'I'll say no more.' She shut her mouth like a mousetrap slamming and poured boiling water on top of the tea bag. She slotted a cigarette into her mouth.

'They're going to make it illegal to smoke soon. Bloody government. Interfering with the rights of the people. If they think I'm going to vote for them they've another think coming. I'd rather emigrate.' She clicked the lighter and a huge flame shot up into the air. She lowered her face towards it and took a deep breath in, pulling the smoke deep down into her lungs. There was silence for a moment and then she coughed. Uh hunh, uh hunh. Uh hunh.

I thought it was time to go.

Uh hunh, uh hunh.

I picked up my bag.

Uh hunh, uh hunh, uh hunh.

'What are you waiting for?'

'I thought maybe you were going to die.'

'Get away out of here and let me get on with my work. Go and see that renegade.'

Yes.

Yes of course. That is what I must do.

✳ ✳ ✳

The traffic was unhelpful, to say the least, and it was quarter past eleven when I drew up at the Bishop's door. It was a blowy day, and I stood outside the door to admire the turbulence of the sea between Howth and Dublin and the streaming white smoke from the tall chimneys and jaunty clouds which seemed to be racing each other across the sky.

The door opened behind me and Mrs Carruthers stood there; she must have been waiting for me in the hall. The wind skittered in around me and the mats in the hall flipped and slithered.

'Come in, why don't you?'

Somewhere a door banged and I stepped quickly into the hall before damage could be done.

'The traffic was awful.'

She nodded. 'The Bishop does not like to be kept waiting.' She walked quickly across the hall. I followed.

'Don't take that tone with me,' I said. 'After all I might not have been able to come at all. Then he'd have had to wait until tomorrow perhaps, or next week.'

She said nothing.

She opened the door to his study and I went in.

He was sitting in his chair by the fire, smoke straggling up the chimney.

'Thank you, Mrs Carruthers. You may bring the coffee now.'

He stared at me as he spoke to her.

I walked across the room and stood in front of him. I didn't know whether to kiss him or not.

'I'm sorry I'm late.'

He nodded and waved a hand towards a chair. 'I have nothing to do but wait,' he said.

He looked thinner and paler than he had on Sunday. His fingers twitched nervously in his lap.

I sat down. In silence we looked at each other.

'How are you?' I asked eventually.

'I am not well. I'm . . .' he paused for a long time considering what words to use '. . . fading. There is a little less of me each day. I have not much time left.'

Behind me the door opened and Mrs Carruthers came in with the tray. He stopped speaking. He gazed towards the fire. She put the tray laden with silver pots and jugs down beside me on a table.

'Will I pour?' she asked.

'That's all right, Mrs Carruthers, I'll do it,' I said and she turned and left the room.

I poured the fine strong, black coffee and brought it over to him.

'Sugar? Cream? Milk?'

He shook his head.

'A scone? There are buttered scones.'

He shook his head again.

I put cream in my own coffee and picked up a warm scone.

'I was not cut out to go into the army or the navy.' He still stared towards the fire, his hand moving from time to time to pick up his cup and carry it shaking to his mouth.

'So.' He sighed a long sigh. 'Willy-nilly it had to be the Church. I suppose I had faith when I used to kneel by my mother's knee and say those little prayers that children say. That children believe. I believed then that He would keep us safe and happy . . . no . . . no, I don't think I knew about happiness then. Safe was the important thing. He had that power. Pretty little prayers that children say. I don't suppose you ever said them. Now I lay me down to sleep. That sort of prayer.'

I shook my head. I knew better than to speak.

The warm scone was delicious; the butter oozed out between my lips and ran down my chin. Mrs Carruthers had also supplied me with a napkin.

'When I reached the age of reason, if you could call it such a title, about sixteen, seventeen, I suppose, I realised that not only was there no God, but that we had invented Him to make sense of this mad world we live in. We had invented this whole scaffolding of lies. Created, I should say, rather than invented, because the artistic breath was what made us believe. The artistic breath gave the stories their glory and their power.'

His voice faltered and he lay back against the chair and closed his eyes. His breathing was anguished. He raised a hand and waved it towards me, a reassuring gesture: I'm waving not drowning. I waited and after a while he opened his eyes and looked at me. I nodded. He sat up again and took a drink of coffee.

'I have only you,' he said.

'Grandfather . . .'

'Don't speak. I don't want you to speak. I want you to listen. When your mother was a child she used to listen to me, but nobody else ever has. You may think that odd, that I should say such a thing. How can he be a bishop if no one has ever listened to him? They listened to the lies I told, they were what they wanted to hear. God lies. Yes. Acting was what I wanted to do. But they wouldn't countenance that. Not for one second. In college I played everything: Shaw, Wilde, Pirandello, Shakespeare. I was good. They got the wind of it. Some friend of theirs saw my Prospero and congratulated them on my performance. I think that to say my father was spitting blood would have been putting it mildly. And my mother cried. I was a fool. Now I can say that, but then I bowed to their pressure and threw myself headlong into my studies. I created my role as curate, rector, dean and finally bishop. I was a masterpiece of deception.' He stopped talking and looked at me. 'What do you think of that?'

'What terrible parents you must have had.'

'No. I don't think they were terrible. They just believed they knew what was best for me.'

'They were wrong.'

'Yes, but they never knew. My father was still alive when I became a bishop. He put his hand on my head and ruffled my hair, like you do to a small child. We were right, boy. Were we not right?'

'What did you say to him?'

'Nothing. What could I say? Thank you, Father, for ruining my life, and my wife's and my . . .'

I waited but he said no more.

He drained his coffee cup.

'More coffee?' I asked. He shook his head.

'I would like to die at peace with myself. I have been musing about such things. I have wondered from time to time about the Romans and their Confession. Is this a sign of health that our Church has disposed of. Absolution. To begin again, clean.'

'You have to believe. You say you don't believe. It's no good, Grandfather, if you don't believe.'

'I know.' His voice was angry. 'I don't need you to tell me that.'

He rubbed fretfully at his forehead with his hand. 'I'm sorry. I don't mean to be . . . I'm sorry . . . I have reproached myself time and again for my . . . my haste to anger.'

'Are you acting now?'

'That is an unkind thing to suggest.'

'You yourself said that you were a master of deception.'

'Yes. You will of course have to decide what to believe and what not. I understand that. I have in the last few days finished writing something which I would like you to read. Take it with you.' He pulled out a bundle of papers from behind the cushion at his back and held it out towards me. 'Please, granddaughter.'

I got up and went over and took the bundle from his hand. He gripped my wrist.

'Please, granddaughter.'

'Yes,' I said. 'I'll read it. Of course I will.'

'And you'll come and see me again.'

I nodded.

He closed his eyes and sank back into the chair.

'You may go now.'

I heard the door behind me open. Mrs Carruthers stood aside to let me through and then followed me along the passage to the hall.

In silence.

In silence she opened the hall door and I stepped out into the sunshine. Without saying a word she closed the door behind me.

The Bishop's recollection

I was married in St Mary's Church, Angelsea Road on 5th May 1943.

The rest of the world was *en plein guerre*.

I had toyed with the idea of enlisting in the British Army, but the more I toyed the more it seemed to me that I would be fighting against Germany, but not for my own country which had chosen to remain neutral in the face of Hitler. To be quite honest I didn't want to go and fight for or against anyone. I considered myself to be a man of peace, but in reality I think I was frightened that I would not be able to cope with the stresses and violences of war.

I had adamantly turned my face away from the theatre and had been ordained in 1940. My parents were pleased with me.

I sang whatever sermons I was asked to give in a

strong, carrying, well-modulated voice. I was a handsome young man, with a hint of anguish in my eyes that intrigued girls, and made my fellow clergy pray for my troubled soul. My stage was now the dwindling Church of Ireland parishes, my audience the anxious ageing parishioners, many of whom had sons and daughters fighting in the war. They were people who at that moment in time had no voice, only the inner whispers that had told them not to leave this country, their country.

Canon Blake's daughter was austere and beautiful, high forehead, long nose, all that sort of stuff. She was their only child and her parents doted on her, but never touched her. 'Well done, my dear,' was the accolade they used most towards her, and having said the words her father would cough and pull his handkerchief from his pocket and blot his forehead. She was silent and well behaved, a shadowy figure just behind her parents wherever they went. If I had become an actor I never would have given her a second thought but as it was I wondered if maybe she was the right person for my invention of myself.

I began to pay her attention. For almost a year we went together to the cinema, once a week, to swim in the summer afternoons out at Dun Laoghaire baths, to tea from time to time with school friends of hers and then one night, after bringing her home from listening to the 'Messiah' in Trinity, outside her hall door, I asked her to marry me.

The rectory had high granite steps up to the door and a small porch reached out over the door itself to shelter people inadequately from the weather. Being almost Christmas there was a sharp wind blowing and as she put up her hand to put the key in the lock I heard myself saying the words.

'I'm going to be a bishop you know.'

She was startled and lowered her hand from the door.

'Not for a few years yet,' she said.

'Oh yes, not for a few years.' I laughed. 'I didn't mean tomorrow.'

Her hand rose again with the key in it.

'I wondered if perhaps . . .'

This seemed wrong suddenly, but I continued.

'. . . we might get married.'

She put the key in the lock and turned it. 'You'd better come in,' she said.

It was almost as cold in the hall as it had been outside. She closed the door behind us and we stood staring at each other. The lamp hanging from the hall ceiling was made of multi-coloured glass and she was blue and green and red.

'What did you say?' she whispered at me.

'I was asking you to marry me. I was proposing to you. I would like you to . . .'

She smiled at me.

'Yes. I'd like that.' It was the most animated smile I had ever seen on her face.

'Really. You really mean that?'

'Yes, of course I mean it.'

I put my hands on her shoulders to draw her to me, to kiss her. Yes, that was what I intended to do, kiss her smiling mouth. I wanted to do that, but the moment my hands touched her she began to shiver and I let her go.

'I . . . I'm sorry.'

'No. You mustn't be.'

She stood on tiptoe and leant towards me. Her mouth brushed my cheek. Like a butterfly, a slight sensation of warmth and then it was gone. Her multi-coloured face trembled. She put out her hand and touched mine, then she turned from me and opened the door again. The wind rushed in.

'You must come around tomorrow and speak to Father.'

I walked past her.

'Yes. I'll do that. Good night.'

'Good night, my dear.'

She closed the door and I was alone

So, on 5th May 1943, we were married, for better for worse, for richer for poorer, in sickness or in health, till death did us part.

Six weeks later the Allies invaded Italy. It seemed like the tide of war was about to change.

The sun shone and we were married by the Archbishop himself and the great and the good of the parish and all our friends and relations were there and after the celebrations were over we set off in a train to the west of Ireland for our honeymoon, our bicycles in the guard's van.

As you might imagine it rained; and that and the difficulty I had trying to persuade my bride that what we were attempting to do together was normal and even enjoyable made our holiday almost intolerable and we returned to Dublin after a week. I suppose now, looking back after all those years, that she was frightened. She had been prepared in no way for marriage. No one had told her what might be expected of her and she had never been filled with the lively curiosity that other girls seemed to have.

My parents had got us a little flat in the top of a house in Upper Baggot Street and there on the first night of our return, under the roof beaten by rain and the streaming windows, I let my desperation get the better of me and I raped her.

She cried.

I felt wretched and angry.

I ran down the stairs and out into the street and walked for three hours and my head was filled with Hamlet and Prospero and the towering Lear that I knew I would never play and their bloody God to whom I had committed my self till death did us part as I had to the snivelling woman back in the flat. I stood at street corners and tears streamed down my cheeks as the rain had streamed down the windows and I longed for my life to end. The rain stopped and the earth became misty and soft and was lit by a half moon and in a tree a bird began to chirp sleepily. The sound woke me up and as I limped home, lights were beginning to flower in the windows of houses and the odd car splashed through puddles on the road; it was the beginning of my new life.

I now knew that I had to become a bishop; it was the only truth that I had spoken to her and I felt it was my duty to follow it through.

I worked hard; it was quite a large parish filled mainly with middle-class, professional people, children to be prepared for confirmation, a few young people wishing to marry and, of course, the poor to be visited, Christmas parties for their children, the youth club to be run and the parish pantomime, a longstanding nightmare. I spared the Canon as much as I could. He smiled upon me and took longer fishing holidays in Connemara; I think he liked me, because I was a good curate but also because I had made his daughter happy. She did appear to be happy. She smiled a lot and helped with parish work, hospital visiting and the annual sale of work in the parish hall in Beaver Row. She called me 'my dear' in public and took my arm; in private we were pretty silent; this silence didn't bother her, but I was lonely, so lonely I could feel my heart beginning to freeze. I knew that soon I would have no feelings left in me. I didn't care.

I have just reread what I have written and I have noticed that not once have I mentioned my wife's name.

Is she Cathie, Joan or Margaret?

Something more exotic perhaps: Madeleine, Natasha, Alexandra?

Or ethnic even: Aoife, Grainne, something like that? I feel I owe her anonymity, the dignity of namelessness.

Maybe if I had loved her even a little she would have become a different person. I doubt it.

Maybe I would have become a different person.

Now there's a thought.

* * *

We seemed to be winning the war at last.

The Allies had landed in Normandy and were fighting their way across the North of Europe. Jokes crept back into people's conversations and their faces became less grey and stressed-looking.

I was in my first parish in West Wicklow, forty families scattered across the hills and low valleys, not badly off; the land was good, their cattle fed well and they were regular church attenders; they came on their bicycles and in their pony traps and brought us butter and fine brown eggs and the odd bottle of poitín.

One summer day she came to me in my study. She crossed the room and sat in the chair opposite my desk. She folded her hands neatly on her knee.

'I think,' she said, 'that it is time we had a child.'

I put down my pen and looked at her. 'Why?'

'I think it is expected of us. My parents are . . . my parents are getting on, you know, and I think . . .'

Her face was red. She stared past me out through the window at the garden.

'You know what this entails, don't you?'

She nodded.

There was a long silence.

'I think you are probably right,' I said at last.

'Thank you.' It was a whisper.

She stood up and came round the desk and stood beside me. She laid a hand on my shoulder and bent and kissed the top of my head.

'Thank you.' She whispered the word again and left the room.

I got up and stood by the window staring out at the bright garden and I longed to be wrapped in the loving arms of God, any God, just someone stronger than I was, someone who loved me without reserve, someone wise and gentle and all-seeing, someone who I knew did not exist.

Almighty God who hast given us grace at this time to make our common supplication unto thee; fulfil now, o Lord, the desires and supplications of thy servants, as may be most expedient for them; granting us in this world knowledge of thy truth and in the world to come life everlasting.

I thought the words in my head.

Clouds crossed the sun and for a moment the garden was grey and then it bloomed again. Shay, the gardener, was working in the border across the lawn; he was kneeling grubbing with his hands, pulling weeds and then smoothing the surface of the earth again. He wore a grey shirt and black trousers and as always a small grey cap was perched on the top of his head, the brim hanging sideways down over his right ear. As he worked he whistled silently, his lips puckered, a slight frown on his forehead.

I wondered if he were a God-fearing man.

An idle thought, but then so many of my thoughts were idle, they still are; even the writing of this memoir is with no greater idea in my head than putting some sort of record straight.

Almighty God, unto whom all hearts be open and from whom no secrets are hid; cleanse the thoughts of our hearts by the inspiration of thy Holy Spirit, that we may perfectly love thee, and worthily magnify thy holy name . . .

Word perfect.

I can still speak each prayer and canticle, each psalm and collect, without recourse to the book of words.

My sermons were masterpieces of clear and inspirational thinking.

I think I can say without modesty that because of me,

because of my appearance of devotion and conviction, many wavering souls drew nearer to God.

What does this make me?

A hypocrite?

Surely that, but the world is very full of them. Not merely priests are hypocrites. Politicians, lawyers, powerful men of business.

Or should I say a liar?

I have lied all my life.

And?

I shall stop writing this now. I must collect my feelings. I must become calm again. I must write my chapters with calm. I must face my truth with calm. I must not falter.

It has taken me two days to find the energy to continue.

I doze; my eyes droop into almost-sleep and my head falls down onto my chest.

Now, today, I feel clearer.

Mrs Carruthers brings me cups of tea and keeps the fire going. I have to say that I do feel the cold so I am grateful for this attention.

I like the girl, Miranda, Sally, the actress.

Yes.

It is for her I write this, though maybe she will end

up hating me. I would like her to understand.

I would like to hold her hand as I go into the darkness.

Anyway enough of that sort of stuff.

It took her about six months to get pregnant. She became more and more anxious as the weeks went by; as did I, I do have to say. I had a vision of myself struggling with her in bed year after year, while nothing happened and we disliked each other more and more. She would lie in the hollow of the bed, her hands clenched, her face white and filled with loathing.

'Go on. Get on. Get on,' she would mutter.

I quoted Shakespeare inside my head.

When in disgrace with fortune and men's eyes
I all alone beweep my outcast state,
And trouble deaf heaven with my bootless cries,
And look upon myself and curse my fate,
Wishing me like to one more rich in hope . . .

So on, so on.

'It should have happened by now.'

'Sometimes it takes years.'

She turned her face away.

'Dear God,' she whispered.

I felt sorry for her then.

After Christmas had passed, when there was a smattering of snow on the ground and the garden looked ragged and mournful, I heard the telephone ringing. I was alone in the house; she had gone into town the day before and had spent the night with her parents in Angelsea Road. I went into the dark hall to answer the telephone.

'Hello.'

'Richard.'

'Oh, hello.'

'I've just come from the doctor. I thought I should tell you first. It's all right. It's happened. You know ... I'm pregnant.'

'That's grand. That's ... I'm so pleased. Yes.' I felt the weight of anxiety rolling off my shoulders, a physical happening, like a cloak slipping from me, removed by kind hands. I stood up straighter than I had for many days.

'Yes. I'm so delighted. For you. For us both. You must take care now. Not do too much.'

'I'll take care. I'll come home this evening. Seven fifteen. My bicycle is at the station.'

'I'll meet you. I have enough petrol. We'll put the bicycle in the boot. You shouldn't go pedalling round in the dark.'

'Thank you. Thank you so much, Richard.'

There was a moment's silence and then the voice of Molly, the postmistress.

'Your three minutes is up, Reverend. I could let you have another minute if you wanted it?'

'Ah, no thanks, Molly. Goodbye, my dear. I'll see you at seven fifteen. Take care.'

'Right so.'

We were disconnected.

*　*　*

Her pregnancy went well. She was obviously the sort of woman who could have had a dozen children without any bother at all, had she so wished. But one was enough for her.

I did not like the thought of her pedalling round the parish on her bicycle any longer, so I bought her a smart little pony trap, which Shay kept clean and in good working order. He enjoyed the company of the pony, a fat twelve-year-old mare of a most benign character, with a rough pale mane and tail and as he brushed and polished her his whistling became louder and sometimes even ecstatic.

I think it was the happiest period of our life together. It was calm. We never rowed. My spiritual problems

were pushed to the back of my mind. Spring drifted
into summer and towards the end of summer she came
to me one day in my study and announced that she was
going to spend the last few weeks of her pregnancy in
Dublin with her parents.

'Mother would like me to be there. It seems sensible.
Just in case.'

'In case of what?'

'Oh, you know. Things can happen. She thinks it
would be better . . .'

'What do you think?'

She looked down at the floor for a moment.

'Yes. I think it would be better. I would feel . . . safer.'

'You must do whatever you want to do.'

I could feel the happiness draining away.

'What does Dr O'Connor think?'

'He thinks I should go. He thinks . . .'

'Yes?'

'I should go.' Her voice was faint.

'What's wrong with the nursing home in Wicklow? I
have petrol saved to bring you in when the time comes.'

'Mother . . .'

'You are the important one. Not your mother. You've
seemed so happy, contented, this last few months.'

'She would like me to go. It's all arranged. I've seen

the doctor there. I've booked in to the nursing home in Hatch Street. I've spoken to Dr O' Connor.'

'You've done all these things, made all these arrangements, without talking to me about it?'

'I thought . . .'

'It's all right, you don't have to tell me. I know what you thought. Go. Of course you must go and have your baby in Dublin. With your mother. Do let me know when it arrives.'

Silly remark. I know that. I knew it as soon as the words blurted out of my mouth. I turned quickly back to my desk.

She stood in silence and looked at me for a while and then went out of the room.

Later that afternoon I watched from the window as Shay put her bags in the trap, the pony whisked her tail as he climbed in and sat waiting, holding the reins. She came into the room and stood by the door. She looked pale and tired.

'I'm off.'

'I would have driven you to the station.'

'It's all right, thank you. You must keep the petrol for parish work. Well, goodbye.'

'Take care of yourself. I will come up and see you next week.'

'You needn't bother.'

I bowed towards her and she ran abruptly from the room.

I watched her leave the house and climb into the trap. Shay leant across her and snapped the door shut, then a flick of the reins on its back and the fat little pony was off down the avenue.

I couldn't see.

It was as if someone had thrown a red blanket over me and I had that colour and nothing else in front of my eyes. I groped my way to the nearest chair and sat with my head in my hands. Breathing was difficult; the blanket was suffocating me as well as blinding me. I must have sat for a long time because I became suddenly aware of the clopping of the pony's hooves as she trotted past the window on her return from the station. I lay back in the chair, exhausted, but breathing and able to see once more.

On the fifteenth of September the child was born.

At ten fifteen in the morning.

At eleven fifteen they telephoned me.

'A lovely little girl,' said my mother-in-law.

I could hear Molly the postmistress's heavy breathing.

'That is wonderful. I'll be up as soon as possible.'

'Nine and a half pounds,' said my mother-in-law.

'Excellent. How is . . .?'

'Tired. Tired but well. It was a seven-hour labour.'

'I will be there this afternoon. Tell her . . .'

'Yes,' said my mother-in-law. 'I'll tell her.'

She put down the receiver.

Molly spoke. 'Reverend . . .'

'Yes, Molly.'

'I couldn't help but hear.'

'That's all right, Molly.'

'Isn't that great now. A lovely little girl.'

'It's great.'

In September flowers are hard to come by in the garden, but I picked what there were: some early chrysanthemums, a few dahlias, and some rosebuds that didn't look as if they would come to anything and Shay filled a box with apples and pears and from the kitchen Nellie appeared with a blackberry tart and I set off for Dublin to see my child. I drove my little car and I sang.

'O be joyful in the Lord all ye lands: serve the Lord with gladness and come before his presence with a song. Be ye sure the Lord he is God: it is he that hath made us and not we ourselves; we are his people and the sheep of his pasture. O go your way into his gates with thanksgiving and into his courts

with praise: be thankful unto him and speak good of his name. For the Lord is gracious, his mercy is everlasting and his truth endureth from generation to generation.'

She was sitting propped among pillows when I went in to see her. Her mother sat on one side of the bed, knitting, and on the other side was a crib with the baby in it. The little creature was fast asleep. Swaddled I felt to within an inch of her life.

I stood and looked down at her for a moment or two.

'May I . . .' I bent towards the baby. I had a very strong desire to hold her, to smell her, to kiss her.

'No.' My wife's voice was strong and slightly shrill. 'No. No. She'll cry if you wake her.'

I looked at my mother in law. She nodded. She pulled a long string of wool from the bag on her knee and wound it round her finger.

'She'll cry.'

'But . . .'

'Next time you come.'

I sat for fifteen minutes with them. Click, click went the knitting needles and the baby snuffled gently.

'We were sure it was going to be a boy. I'm sorry it's not . . .'

'I'm not.'

'Wouldn't you have preferred a . . .?'

'No. We haven't discussed names.'

'Ruth. Just Ruth. Nothing else.'

'Oh.' I was a little taken aback by the firm tone of her voice. 'Ruth's a good name. I would have no quibbles with that. Shouldn't she have another name though?'

'I see no need to be wasteful with names.' She closed her eyes.

I stood up.

'Is there anything that you need? Any shopping? Books? Anything at all?'

'Mother can do those things for me.'

'I have the car . . .'

'You must save the petrol for bringing us home.'

'Yes.'

I went out into the passage and closed the door behind me.

Ruth.

The smell of floor polish and disinfectant.

Ruth.

A nurse walked swiftly past me, her feet squeaking on the polished floor.

Ruth.

When I got her to myself I would examine every

part of her. I would unwrap her from her swaddling and touch her and kiss her and stroke her, do all the things that lovers do, and she would open her toothless mouth and smile at me.

My Ruth.

I moved down the passage and out into Hatch Street. A little wind blew papers along the street.

I would know her as I had known no one else; I would love her. Everything that was good in me would be poured out in front of her; I promised that.

I almost ran along Leeson Street and crossed the wide road without looking to left or right. I cut through the corner of the Green; the trees were beginning to turn and a few leaves fluttered on the paths, multi-coloured, flexible in the early autumn breeze. Women knitted and gossiped on the seats and their children played on the grass nearby.

Ruth.

What, I wondered, would I have called her had I had a say in the matter?

I came out of the gate at the top of Dawson Street and waited as a tram swung round the corner. It didn't matter; she was Ruth. I have met a person called Ruth; a person I love with all my heart.

I walked down Dawson Street, past the Mansion

House and went into St Anne's Church. It was dark, just one or two lights were on, and I sat down in the front pew and closed my eyes.

> *'The voice I hear this passing night was heard*
> *In ancient days by emperor and clown:*
> *Perhaps the self-same song that found a path*
> *Through the sad heart of Ruth, when sick for home,*
> *She stood in tears amid the alien corn;*
> *The same that oft-times hath*
> *Charm'd magic casements, opening on the foam*
> *Of perilous seas, in faery lands forlorn.'*

I must unknowingly have spoken the words aloud as there was a rustling and a hand was laid on my shoulder.

'Richard.'

Startled, I looked up to find the Rector standing beside me. He and I had been in college together.

'Oh— I—' I began to rise to my feet, but his hand remained on my shoulder, pushing me back down into my pew.

'My dear fellow, don't move. I just wondered if you were all right.'

He was wearing his cassock and a large silver cross hung around his neck.

'I heard you come in. We've just had a baptism and I was just checking that everything was shipshape again. Shipshape. Are you all right? I got the feeling that maybe . . .' He paused and stared into my face. 'You were distressed in some way.'

'No. No, no. Quite the opposite. I have just become a father. My wife has . . . Ruth. The child is called Ruth. I . . . ah just felt I should . . .' I raised my hands and my eyes towards the roof.

He nodded his approbation. 'Good man.' His hand left my shoulder. 'Splendid. I congratulate you. Yes. Such a happy occasion. Don't stir yourself. I have to run. I have to go to the celebration. Brown will be pottering in before dark, turning off lights, locking doors, that sort of thing. So don't rush out. Speak to God. Yes. Take all the time you need. Good man.'

He put out a hand and I shook it.

'Thank you,' I muttered, feeling fraudulent.

He turned from me and seemed to melt into the darkness. I closed my eyes once more.

'I renounce the devil and all his works, the vain pomp and glory of the world, with all covetous desires of the same, and the sinful desires of the flesh, so that I will not follow nor be led by them.'

I got up and bowed towards the altar and went out into the windy street.

Ruth, I will love you for ever.

* * *

They came home after about three weeks and a nice rosy-cheeked girl from the village was employed to help with the baby. From my study I used to watch her push the pram round the garden paths until the baby had gone to sleep, then she would carefully park the pram under a tree and run off to do whatever chores there were for her to do.

When she had disappeared from view I would open the door and step out onto the grass, then walking with all silence so as not to disturb the sleeping child I would cross the distance between my room and the tree and stand looking down at Ruth. She grew quite quickly into beauty and as I stood and watched her sleep I felt my heart was going to burst with love and pride. One morning, she must have been about five months old, she opened her eyes and saw me standing over her. She smiled and put up a hand towards me; I leant forward and let her take my finger. She held it tightly as if it were the one thing in the world that she longed for and in a twinkling of an eye she was asleep again. I stood there for a while, my finger in her hand. A voice called something and then called again.

'Richard.'

I didn't answer. I just stood there looking down at the baby; her fingers were creamy and long and curled round my finger, her grip strong.

'Richard.'

She was calling from her bedroom window.

'For heaven's sake, don't wake the child.'

Gently I pulled my finger from her hand and moved away from the pram. I walked slowly across the grass towards my room.

'I wouldn't do that,' I called.

'She needs to sleep undisturbed.'

I went into the house and closed the door.

I seldom had the chance to see her alone. Always there was someone else there, or in and out of the room. I kissed her warm cheeks and blew warm air in her ears and on her fingers. In return she laughed and pulled my hair or tried to snatch my glasses from my nose.

'This little piggy went to market, this little piggy stayed at home.'

She loved that and also:

'This is the way the ladies ride, trit trot, trit trot.
This is the way the gentlemen ride. Canter, canter,
canter.
And this is the way the big farmer rides. Gallopy,
gallopy, gallopy, down into the big hole he tumbles.'

She loved being thrown gently in the air and caught again and thrown and caught until the voice spoke.

'That's enough now, Richard. You'll make her sick.'

There was always the restraining voice.

The hands that lifted her firmly from my knee and whisked her away back into the world of women.

She learnt so fast, Ruth; she learnt to stretch out her arms to me. 'Da da da,' she would say. She learnt how to clap her hands and how to pucker up her soft lips for a kiss. I could see no wrong in her.

'I think that Susan will have to go.'

My wife and I were having lunch.

'Why? She seems a nice enough girl to me.'

'I don't like her red cheeks. They're too red. Mother says it looks like ... you know what.'

'You know what?'

'TB. It's a sign. We wouldn't want anything like that around Ruth.'

'Have you asked her? Have you made enquiries?'

She bowed her head silently.

I knew what she meant; she hadn't and nor was she going to.

'It's up to you,' I said. 'I find her very satisfactory. Ruth seems to like her.'

'Ruth is too young to know.'

'She's kind.'

'If she has TB . . .'

'She just has rosy cheeks.'

'Mother . . .'

'Your mother . . .'

'She has heard her cough.'

'I bow to your mother's instinct. So what do you intend to do? You will mind the child yourself? Is that what you want to do?'

'Mother   '

I did sigh noisily at that moment.

'Mother has found someone for us. A real nanny. A middle-aged woman with experience. A . . . a . . . Protestant.'

'Oh good. How kind of your mother.' I clicked my knife and fork together and stood up. 'Yes, yes. I see. We have been most negligent in not protecting our baby from the Romans. Your mother is a worthy watchdog. Thank her from me.' I walked to the door and then turned and looked at her. She looked a little flustered. 'Don't worry, my dear, Ruth's soul will be in good hands and she won't get TB.'

The nanny was a nice enough woman with curly greying hair and a hearty laugh. She sang different songs to Ruth.

> *Just a song at twilight*
> *When the lights are low*
> *And the flickering shadows*
> *Softly come and go.'*

She played the piano, just simple chords.

> *'There was an old woman, as I've heard tell;*
> *Fa la lalalalala.*
> *And she went to market her eggs for to sell;*
> *Fa la lalalalala.'*

She would set the baby on her knee and play and Ruth would thump with her fists and chuckle, and I would creep from my study and stand in the drawing-room door and watch them.

> *'She went to market, on a market day,*

Fa la lalalalala
And she fell asleep by the king's highway;
Fa la lalalalala.'

When the song was ended she would swing round on
the stool and say, 'Now, clap hands. Clap hands for
Mamma, clap hands for Daddy and then away off to bed
we go.'

I can hear her voice chanting now across the years.

'The minstrel boy to the war has gone,
In the ranks of death you'll find him.
His father's sword he has girded on,
And his wild harp slu . . . u . . . ung behind
him.'

She enjoyed the garden, and on summer afternoons, she
would take off her white starched apron and kneeling
by the herbaceous border she would weed the bed,
while Ruth sat beside her on a rug or crawled on the
grass, picking daisies and holding them up to the sky in
triumph.

I'm afraid I wasted my time by watching them both.

She stayed with us for five years and then insisted
that her usefuness was over.

'I must go to a house where there is a baby. Babies are my strong point. So, much as I love Ruth, I must go. She'll be at school now and what would I be doing with myself?'

There was no changing her mind. Off she went, in the middle of summer, to a young solicitor and his wife who lived in Cabinteely and had just had their first baby. Ruth cried every evening when she went to bed. I could hear her and one evening I went into her room. Her head was buried in her pillows. I sat down beside her and put my hand on her shoulder. She turned over and looked me; her eyes were red and tears streaked down her cheeks.

'I want Nanny.'

'I'm sorry, darling, but she had to go.'

'Why? She loved me. She said she loved me.'

'You're too old for a nanny. You're going to school in September. After all she couldn't stay for ever.'

'Why not?'

'Here.' I handed her my handkerchief. 'Mop up. Nannies don't stay for ever. You've got Mummy and me. We love you too, you know. We will never leave you. You will grow up and leave us. That's the way things go.'

'Why couldn't we get another baby, then she would come back to us?'

'We can't do that, darling.'

'Why not?'

'We just can't. We'll have to learn to live without her. In a week or so everything will be all right.'

She put her arms up and pulled my head down towards her face and held me there. Her cheeks were hot and soft.

I held her close to me and rocked her in my arms. She seemed happy to be there.

'You have buttons,' she whispered at one moment and then fell asleep. I held her for a few minutes, then I gently kissed her cheek and tucked her back into her bed again. I stood looking down at her until I heard her mother calling me, then I tiptoed out of the room.

'Where have you been?'

'She was crying.'

'I didn't hear her.'

'Nonetheless . . . She is missing Nanny.'

'She'll have to get used to that. You mustn't spoil her. Nanny spoiled her enough, heaven knows. Mother says it's a good thing that she left.'

'It was your mother's idea that she come.'

'Yes. But enough's enough. She's going to have to learn to love me now and do what I tell her.'

She turned and walked away down the passage.

* * *

I used to take Ruth to school each morning in the car; the war was well over and we had petrol for this sort of extravagance.

It was a small Church of Ireland school next to the church with two teachers. I would walk to the door with her each day, my hand lightly resting on her shoulder, and shake the hand of whichever teacher was standing by the door.

' 'Bye Ruth. Be a good girl,' and she was gone.

'Good morning, Rector. Isn't she always good? Good as gold.'

My eyes would follow her as she made a beeline for her friends.

The time came when instead of me reading to her, she would read to me, her finger following the lines of words along the page. Soon she read with fluency and with heart.

Sometimes, if her mother allowed it, she would come with me on my parish visits, up into the heart of the mountains, where there was still no electricity and the dogs yapped and snarled around the legs of strangers. She liked these jaunts and would lean out of the window as we drove taking in deep breaths of the piney mountain air. Sometimes we would stop by the side of a small lake and she would take off her shoes and socks and paddle for a minute or two in the brown water. I did that once also, being seduced by the heat of the sun, but the water was so cold I never tried it again, preferring to sit on the grass and watch her and listen to her small screams of pain and delight as she slithered on the slippery pebbles that bordered the lake.

Of course all good things have to come to an end and when she was about twelve I was moved to Dublin to a large church in Harold's Cross, with a surprisingly large congregation of working-class men and women.

It was beleaguered; as young city people mix more with each other than they do in the country and in the dance halls as well as in the workplaces Catholics met Protestants and fell in love. *No Tomoro* was decimating the Church of Ireland: I was determined to stop the rot as best I could.

Dear Sally, if you want to know of my successes and failures in this area of my life, my thunderings and cajolings, my reasoned arguments, you must read my memoirs. You should probably read them anyway, the story of my rise and rise in a job in which I lied till I was blue in the face, and everyone thought that I spoke the truth; well, almost everyone.

Ruth went to Alexandra School, at that time still in a row of red-brick houses in Earlsfort Terrace opposite UCD.

Round the corner in Leeson Street was the Sacred Heart Convent and opposite to it CUS for boys and along the road in Stephen's Green the Dominican Convent; altogether a wonderful educational corner of the city!

Ruth pedalled off each morning in her brown uniform, her satchel strapped on her back. Her mother had wanted me to drive her, but the girl insisted on being allowed to use her bicycle. As she turned out of the rectory gate at half past eight each morning, she would wave to me and blow me a kiss and I would, inside my head, call out to her, 'Go in peace, dear child.'

Peace was my password at that time, or perhaps I should say pastime; I spoke sermons on the subject, peace between nations, between religions, between families; I spoke at meetings around the country, not very well attended I do have to say, I spoke at the Synod, and I wrote articles in newspapers and periodicals recommending peace in every walk of life. I would bless my congregations with the words:

'Grace be unto you, and peace, from Him which is, and which was, and which is to come.'

Unorthodox, some people said, and others did not seem to notice. No one complained.

They made me a canon and when my father-in-law retired to spend his last years fishing in Connemara, I became Rector of St Mary's in Angelsea Road and we went to live in the house where my wife had grown up.

I worked hard and I watched my daughter grow from a child into a beautiful girl. In October 1961 Ruth had just turned sixteen; she had successfully passed her Inter exam and was beginning to work for her Leaving. Her mother wished her to go to Oxford, get out of the country, broaden her horizons, meet new people; on and on she would go while Ruth stared out of the window and refused to speak.

'That child is hopeless,' her mother said to me one day. 'She simply refuses to understand that what I want for her is the best. The best. You must talk to her.'

I shook my head.

'I think she must make her own decision. Don't nag on at her.'

'I don't nag.'

'It seems to me that you do, perpetually.'

'I do not nag. She never listens to a word I say.'

'No children of her age listen to their parents.'

'How on earth can a child of her age make the right

decisions about her future. Her whole life. She knows nothing. She has no experience. She should at least try and get into Oxford. Mother says . . .'

I sighed.

'Your mother—'

'My mother knows what she is talking about. Uncle Harry went to Oxford, and my grandfather.'

'Yes. Yes, I know. You've told me a thousand times.'

'And you haven't listened a thousand times. You are her father. You must speak to her. Tell her.'

'Tell her what?'

'What she must do. In her own interests. That is what you must impress on her. Her own interests.'

She stared at me for a long time; finally I bowed my head.

'As you wish.'

A few days later I spoke to Ruth; her mother was out when she came home from school. I put my head round the door of my study.

'Ruth. A moment, if you don't mind.'

She took off her coat and threw it on a chair and came into my room. A fire in the grate was smoking rather disagreeably.

'Oh God, Dadda, that's horrible. Why don't you get the chimney cleaned?'

'It'll be all right in a few minutes. It always smokes when it's first lit. Look, what I have to say...'

'You needn't bother. I know. I know, I know.'

She kicked at the pathetic coal in the fireplace, then she turned and looked me in the eyes.

'It's going to be more of the same, isn't it. Well, I'm sick of it from her. Up till now you've kept out of it. Could you just not let it be?'

'I promised...'

'OK. Shoot.' She threw herself into the armchair by the fire and stuck her fingers in her ears. I walked over to the window and looked across our garden at Ailesbury Road; it was a road I had never liked. Its high red-brick houses seemed like prisons to me, out of which at quarter to nine every morning stepped men in hats, carrying rolled umbrellas, out on day release, earning big money to support their families. As I watched they were coming home, back to their prisons, slightly hunched beneath their umbrellas, their feet weary with having been neatly placed on the carpet beneath their desks all day. Very few of them belonged to my congregration. I don't know how long I watched for before her voice disturbed me.'

'Dadda.'

'Hmm? What? Oh, yes.'

She was standing at my shoulder.

'You haven't said a word.'

'No.'

'For ages. I sat and sat and you said nothing.'

'I'm sorry.'

She put her arm around my neck and kissed my cheek. Then she put her hand on my chin and turned my face to her; gently she kissed my lips.

'Dear Dadda,' she whispered. Then she whirled away, feet tapping and arms outstretched, round and round the room, finally throwing herself back into her chair again. I was dizzy from watching her.

I was dizzy from watching her.

I sat down, shaking.

I was dizzy . . .

I cleared my throat.

'I give you my word,' I said. 'Yes, yes. You do not have to go to university in England, unless you want to. You do not have to . . .'

She laughed. 'I bet that's not what she told you to say.'

I shook my head.

'You mean it?'

'Of course.'

'I can go to Trinity and read law? That's what I want to do, Dadda.'

'My dear child, your future is in your own hands.'

'Mummy . . .'

'It's the first few steps that are the most difficult. I never had the courage to take them. I would hate to see you in the same boat. Don't worry about your mother. I will take care of her.'

Words are so easy to say. If we could foresee the future would we ever speak at all?

I said to her mother what I had said to Ruth and she let a cold curtain of silence fall between us. She also hardly spoke to Ruth. There were no smiles or laughter in the house. Ruth no longer invited her friends home, and I have to say I missed the sounds of their footsteps on the stairs and the muffled giggles that used to come from her room, I missed the energy they used to bring with them.

My father-in-law began to die. He got weaker and more helpless as the weeks went by and finally one morning my wife came to me in my study.

'I must go to Mother,' she said. 'Can you take me to the Galway train?' Her eyes were filled with tears.

'Of course I can. When do you want to go? Do you want me to drive you all the way?'

'No. I mean no thank you. Mother would only worry if you were there. I must go so that she can get some rest. Thank you though. I don't think it will be for very long.' She pulled a handkerchief from her pocket and wiped at her eyes. 'Just to the station.'

'When?'

'I said I'd catch the one o'clock train.'

'We should leave here at twelve.'

'Thank you.'

What was the name of the station then? Kingsbridge? Heuston? I don't remember. Anyway for some reason or other it was jammed with people; hurrying, standing, pulling cases on little wheels, standing in queues, saying goodbye, saying hello. I parked the car in the taxi rank, and hoped that my dog collar would earn me a fool's pardon. I bought her a first-class ticket and saw her onto the train. I put her case on the rack and stooped and kissed her cheek. She nodded and touched my hand.

'Don't wait. Richard.'

'Yes.'

'Don't let the child run wild while I'm away.'

'Please give my regards to your mother.'

I climbed down onto the platform. For a moment I stood there smiling at her, then she took her book from her bag and began to read.

* * *

He lasted two weeks, the old man, drifting painlessly into the vast sea of death. Attended, tended, turned and soothed by his wife and daughter; always one of them was there with him; always, when he opened his eyes, he saw a familiar face hanging in the air beside his bed.

> *'Lord, now lettest thou thy servant depart in peace: according to thy word. For mine eyes have seen thy salvation, which thou hast prepared before the face of all people; to be a light to lighten the gentiles; and to be the glory of thy people Israel.'*

They would whisper the words softly and sometimes his mouth would open and shut soundlessly. They knew he could hear and understand them. Some days he was burning with a fever and others cold and pale as if he were already dead. He refused all food, clamping his thin lips together and shaking his head from side to side when they put the spoon to his mouth.

All these things she told me afterwards and sad grey tears drizzled down her cheeks as she spoke.

* * *

For the first week after my wife's departure for the west Ruth and I hardly saw each other; we passed on the stairs or in the hall like shadows with no weight or substance. If we ate together, we ate in silence or just shuffled meaningless words from our mouths. Then one night as I was passing the door of her room on my way to bed, I heard the sound of crying. I stood for a few moments with my hand on the knob, listening and wondering what I should do. Gently I turned the knob and went in. She was bundled on the bed, her head buried in the pillows; she didn't hear me cross the room. I stood looking down at her for a long time and then sat down on the bed. I put my hand out and touched her shoulder. My fingers crept beneath her hair and stroked her neck; it was warm and slightly damp. Across her shoulders were four brown moles which I had never seen before; I circled each one with a finger. Her sobbing stopped and she reached out a hand and placed it on my knee. I stared at the moles; her skin was the colour of Jersey cream. My fingers were shaking so I moved my hand from her back and placed it gently on her hand that lay on my knee. I closed my eyes.

'Dear child.' My voice was shaking too, but she didn't seem to notice. 'What is the matter? Tell me.'

She threw her arms around me, her face pressed into my waistcoat. She was wrapped in a bath towel.

'I can't bear to see you so unhappy. Please tell me. Please, please, please, my darling girl.'

'Dadda.'

'My darling girl.'

'Oh Dadda, Dadda.'

Such incoherence seemed quite natural. I had so seldom in my life called anyone darling; now it was delicious, a magical word. I couldn't stop.

'Darling.'

'No one loves me.'

'Of course they do. We do. Your friends ... we all do.'

'Mummy hates me.'

'No, no my darling, of course she doesn't, she just wants what she thinks is the best for you. You are so special. She wants ... she wants a very special future for you.'

'No, she doesn't. She wants me to be her poodle. She wants me to do what she hadn't the guts to do. She wants to be me. To live her life through me. That's not loving someone, that's owning someone. When I don't do what she wants, she hates me.'

'No, no, no.'

'Yes, she does. I know the look in her eyes, they go grey and cold.'

She looked up at me, right into my eyes; I felt the strength of her look in my guts. She put up a hand and touched my face, my cheek, then up the side of my left eye and then across my forehead, her gentle fingers.

Her gentle fingers.

Her gentle . . .

I forced myself to laugh.

'Why are you laughing, Dadda?'

'It's the buttons.'

'Buttons?'

'Yes, your cheek. My waistcoat buttons . . .'

'Your stupid buttons. Why do you wear such stupid . . .?' In a frenzy she began to unbutton my waistcoat and the towel slipped from round her and I saw her breasts.

'You're shaking, Dadda.'

'Yes. I'm afraid.'

She pulled off my jacket and waistcoat and began to unfasten my shirt.

'Afraid?'

'Yes.'

'Of me?'

Her fingers brushed the skin of my chest and my stomach and I groaned. I tried not to but the sound burst out of me willy-nilly.

She laughed. 'You must not be afraid of me. I love you, Dadda. I adore you. Do you love me? Please. Do you?'

I put my hands in her hair and pulled her face towards me.

I will kiss her. I will have that pleasure. Then it will be over. Then I will stop. I will show her by kissing her how much I love her. Her heart was beating against mine, she was so warm. It had been so long and never before like this.

Never.

I can't breathe.

'Darling.'

'Darling.'

I can't see. Her hair is in my eyes.

Her breath is in my mouth, sweet minty breath. I have forgotten how to do this.

'No.' It is my voice.

'Please, Dadda. Please show. Teach me about loving. Love me. Oh Dadda.'

'No.' That stupid voice again.

I push myself up from the bed, but her arms entwine me. Pull me down against her warm creamy body.

'Teach. Love me.'

And I am lost in her youth and warmth and my terrible need.

She went asleep curled into my arms and I lay for a while exhausted and frightened by the happiness that filled me. I lay like that for about an hour; my heart's hammering had become a gentle rhythmic knock. Then I crept from the bed and collected my scattered clothes. I tucked her in, smoothing the sheets and blankets like a mother would, then bent and kissed her hair.

Back in my room I fell onto my bed, I got up and walked backwards and forwards, backwards and forwards over the floor. I looked at my forty-five-year-old body in the pier glass and hated it; I walked on, came back once more to the glass; this time I was almost in love with my own appearance. I was exhilarated, I was exhausted, I was in despair, I was happiness, just, total happiness, my whole being filled with joy. I had never felt that way before and then all of a sudden, like falling into a huge hole . . . a cavern, everything was black. I couldn't see my way. Will I ever see my way again?

My head throbbed with the confusion in it. I threw open the curtains and pressed my forehead against the cold glass.

I could see the road below me, empty, dark but for the splashes of light from the street lamps and in the light the swaying branches of the trees seemed to dance in the early morning breeze.

I was sitting in the dining room eating my breakfast when she came in, running as usual. She was in her brown uniform, knee socks, her hair in long plaits hanging down past her shouders; she looked like a child. She put an arm round my neck and kissed my cheek.

'Morning, Dadda.'

She poured herself a cup of tea and grabbed a piece of toast.

'Ruth . . .'

'Rushing, rushing, no time for talk, see you this evening. 'Bye.'

With her cup in one hand and the toast in the other she ran out of the door, pausing just long enough to say, 'I love you,' and then she was gone.

What had I been about to say to her?

Offer some abject apology?

Say something quite banal as if nothing had happened. 'Sit down and eat your breakfast properly?'

Mention God?

Why would I do that?

Maybe to her the name of God might mean something, maybe not.

I decided to go to my church and sit in the silence there and collect my thoughts. It was a blustery day and the wind buffeted me all the way down Angelsea Road; it clutched at my clothes and my hair; it seemed to be unfastening my buttons as she had done. I pulled my coat close around me and walked very fast.

'O Lord, our heavenly father, almighty and everlasting God, who hast safely brought us to the beginning of this day; defend us in the same with thy mighty power; and grant that we fall into no sin, neither run into any kind of danger; but that all our doings may be ordered by thy governance, to do always that which is righteous in thy sight.'

The collect for Grace.

I whispered it and the words filled my head and pushed out all thought, so I whispered it again and again. I knelt at the communion rail, as close as I could get to the seat of God. And I whispered it again. Her skin had been so soft and she had wanted me, as I had wanted her, soft and smooth and her teeth and tongue delicious. I whispered the words again and again and the image of my child was before my eyes.

What was Grace if not that picture?

Grace was in my child.

Righteousness was in my child.

We are not sinners.

My child is not a sinner.

* * *

That evening I ate my dinner alone; I telephoned my wife in Connemara as I usually did.

The old man was now unconscious; his death was only a matter of time, tonight, perhaps, tomorrow, who could say? There was a nurse there with them now, at night.

'Things happen at night,' she whispered down the phone.

'Yes. Do you want me to come down now?'

'No. Wait.'

'I'll come if you would like me to.'

'No. Wait.' Her voice was sharp.

'As you wish.'

'How is Ruth?'

'Fine. She seems to be fine.'

'Is she there now.'

'No. I think she must be having supper with friends.'

'She shouldn't go out on week nights. You know that.'

'She won't be late . . .' As I spoke the words I heard her feet running up the stairs. As she passed me she ran her fingers along the back of my neck and I gasped with shock and pleasure.

'Ahhh.'

'What? What? I didn't hear you.'

'Nothing, my dear. Just a little tickle in my throat.'

'Well, don't let that child stay up too late. Good night.'

'Good night.'

I put down the receiver and stood in the dark hall, I heard her little laugh and then her door close. I was shaking.

I had never before, as far as I could remember, been a vain man, but that evening, I pulled the curtains tight and bathed and shaved, I cut my nails and pulled at my hair and cut recalcitrant strands of it with the nail scissors. I found a bottle of eau de cologne in the bathroom cupboard and rubbed some on my neck and shoulders. Nothing, I thought sadly to myself as I stood in front of the glass, made up for youth. I put on my dressing gown and went across the landing to her room.

She lay, partly covered by the sheet, her hair like a veil over her shoulders. She held out her arms to me.

'I thought you were not going to come.'

'How could you think such a thing?'

I was standing by her; she put out a hand and pushing aside my dressing gown touched me.

'No buttons tonight.'

Her fingers were like butterflies.

For three days and three nights we were like ecstatic children living in some paradise world; she went to school as usual and I worked, I visited my parishioners, I wrote a piece for the *Irish Times*, I had lunch with the Archbishop, I interviewed a young man who wished to become my curate and I had time to slip into town and lay out a lot of money on a bottle of Pour Hommes, which I felt would be more appropriate than the eau de cologne from the bathroom cupboard.

'How beautiful you smell,' she said, nuzzling my shoulder with her nose. 'Yesterday you smelled like Mummy.'

A sharp nip that from the dragon's tooth!

On the morning of the fourth day the telephone rang as I was having my breakfast. It was my wife.

'He's gone.' Her voice was full of tears. 'He went last night, but I didn't want to disturb you. After all what could you have done last night? He just slipped away in his sleep. Mother knew. We were both there with him, she knew. She just suddenly said, "He's gone." Just like that and she was right. It was all very peaceful.'

She blew her nose and I knew at that moment that the end of the world for me had come.

'I am so sorry. But it was quick and peaceful. How is your mother?'

'I sent her to bed. The nurse gave her hot milk and a sleeping pill. Nurse and I are . . . are . . .'

'I'll come at once. I sh . . . we should be able to leave in about half an hour. We should be with you by lunchtime. You go to bed too, my dear. I'm sure you're exhausted.'

'I'm all right, Richard. I have energy. I can keep going.'

'Just take care of yourself. I'll see you soon.'

I went back into the dining room. Ruth was sitting at the table eating toast and marmalade.

'Your grandfather is dead. That was your mother on the phone. I told her we would be down by lunchtime.'

'Poor old pet. He was such a nice gentle old man. I always used to feel he wanted to pick me up and hug me, but no one would let him. He didn't dare do it off his own bat.'

She blew her nose in her napkin. She rubbed the corner of her eye with a finger. 'He used to give me little tubes of fruit pastilles, slip them into my pocket without anyone knowing. I never thought he would die. Just be old and sweet forever.' She put her hands over her face and began to cry.

I stood behind her and held her shoulders; they were the fragile shoulders of a child.

'I didn't think that anyone would die.' She turned and pressed her face against my chest. I held her tight.

'Don't die, Dadda. Don't die on me. Please, please.'

'Of course I won't. Why would I do a thing like that? Here.'

I gave her my handkerchief.

She blew and mopped and rubbed.

'Buttons again.'

Her cheek was covered with button marks.

'Come, eat your breakfast, dear girl. We have to get on the road. I must ring the school and let them know you won't be there. I must tell Annie and I must try and find someone to take the services on Sunday. Then we must go. Yes.' I gulped some tea. 'Yes.'

So an hour later we turned out of the gate. Annie had made us some sandwiches and a thermos of tea.

'Just in case,' she said as she put them into my hands. 'You never can tell what might or might not happen. It's as well to have a bite to eat.' She stood just inside the gate and watched us drive off.

We drove in total silence all the way; even when we stopped by the side of the road to eat Annie's sandwiches we didn't speak. We didn't even look at each other. The joy of the last few days had gone and we were each left with the enormity of what had happened.

We knew that nothing would ever be the same again.

She sat erect beside me, her hands clasped lightly on her lap, and stared out of the windscreen. It was a turbulent day, with huge clouds chasing each other across the sky, moments of brilliant sunshine and then the nearer we got to the west rain spilled on us out of nowhere.

We drew up outside the house and I switched off the engine; we sat in the car, unmoving, staring out at the escallonia hedge in front of us.

'I'm sorry,' I said at last. 'Please forgive me. Please.'

'No. How can I ever do that?' It was a granite voice, hard and intolerable.

I put out my hand to her and she flinched away.

'No. Don't ever touch me again. Ever, as long as either of us live. You are perverted, filthy, and I hate you.'

The hall door opened and her mother appeared.

'Your mother.'

Ruth jumped out of the car and slammed the door; she ran, it seemed, to the protection of her mother.

'Mummy. I'm sorry, so, so sorry.'

They both stood and then without a word they went into the house, arms around each other, and I wondered if her mother understood what Ruth was talking about.

Of course not.

*'I will arise and go to my father, and will say
unto him, Father I have sinned against heaven and
before thee and am no more worthy to be called
thy son.'*

Trippingly off the tongue the words came.

I took the cases out of the car and followed the two
women into the house. The local Rector, a mild and
gentle man called Patterson, and I committed the old
man's body to the ground.

*'I know that my redeemer liveth, and that he shall
stand at the latter day upon the earth: and though,
after my skin, worms destroy this body, yet in my
flesh shall I see God.'*

I spoke the words in my best voice and they filled the
church in their splendour. Ruth, her mother and grandmother stood dry-eyed in the front pew; among the
others there was a smattering of tears.

The sexton tolled the cracked bell and we shuffled to
the graveside. The rain held off and a soft breeze blew
our clothes and our hair and we didn't linger very long.

* * *

'Mother cannot possibly stay here on her own.'

'I agree. It's remote . . . She's . . .'

We were standing outside the house, looking down the hill and across Clew Bay, one of the landscapes that I have always loved best. I had been considering the bay and its burden of islands, stamping them on my mind; my bag was packed and in the car Ruth sat stony-faced in the front seat, impatient to be gone.

'I thought we should have her to stay . . . for a while, until she feels more able to cope. What do you think?'

'Of course. Absolutely. She will be welcome to stay.'

'It will be like going home for her. I really feel it's her house, that we are her visitors.'

'You must do as you think fit.'

'Yes. Yes. I'll let you know when we've sorted things out here and you might come and collect us?'

'I can do that. Just let me know.'

She patted my shoulder and walked over to the car. She bent down and looked in the window at Ruth. 'Granny and I will be home soon. Be good for your father. Keep the work up to the mark.'

Ruth nodded.

'We'll see you soon. Goodbye. Goodbye, Richard.'

✳   ✳   ✳

It was getting dark when we arrived home. No word had been spoken on the drive. She again sat bolt upright, her hands lightly clasped on her knee. I can see her now, the coldness gathering round her. She took her case from the back of the car and carried it up the steps; at the door she turned to me. 'We can't live any more in the same house. You do understand that, don't you?'

'Ruth . . .'

'I will go away.'

'No.'

'I will go away, Dadda, and you must promise me that you will not . . . not look for me. You must promise . . . or let her look for me. I have thought hard about this for the last three days and I know what I must do. I am bright. I am healthy. I can lie like a trooper and I will go to England.' She smiled for a moment. 'Our dustbin, it's funny after all the talk and rows about university and all that sort of thing, that I will take the mail boat, the garbage transporter. But, I'll make it. You don't have to worry about me. I'll survive.'

'Don't be so ridiculous. My darling girl . . . you mustn't even think of going away . . .'

She held her hand out towards me.

'The key. Give me the key. I'm going. My mind's made up. The key, Dadda, please give me the key.'

I found the key and held it out to her; she snatched it from me.

'I really hate you so much. I just want you to know that. I hate you.'

She put the key in the lock and went into the house.

I was shivering so much I could barely stand. I leant against the wall; it must have been about fifteen minutes before I had my body under control and was able to step into the hall and close the door. I went into my study and knelt down by my desk and tried to pray to God.

'If you exist,' I knew I was starting on the wrong foot. 'Please help us now. Manifest yourself to me. You will find no better servant than I will be. Don't take her away from me.' I knew it was hopeless; I had no words. I had no faith. I had no power over my daughter to make her stay. It was dark and quite silent; only the shadows of the trees moved in the light from the street lamps.

I still dream of that night, of the dancing trees and the silence that has been with me ever since, the true beginning of my wretchedness.

She went as she said she would. I went to Connemara to bring her mother home, and her grandmother, and when we came back she was gone. Her room was empty, her clothes, her books, her bits and pieces all gone. She had made a good plan. Her mother, of course, blamed me, but not for the right reasons: my incompetence, my capacity for spoiling the child, they were in her mind.

'You gave her money so that she could go?' she shouted at me.

Her mother hovered in the background; her mother was to hover in the background until her death five years later.

'No.'

'You must get her back.'

'No.'

'What will I say to people?'

'Just say she's gone to England.'

'You gave her money.'

I left them standing in the hall, their bags and bundles around their feet, looking like a pair of refugees.

I, though, became the refugee in my own house after that. I shut myself in my study, I slipped through the hall and out the door, when I knew no one was there to see me. I ate silently with the women, who seldom threw a word in my direction; they treated me in fact like some unwanted guest who had outstayed his welcome.

I had of course put money in her bank, which I

continued to do, and which she used; she made no grand gestures towards rejecting the money. I had at least that security.

I always hoped that she would telephone me, or write, but she did neither. I presumed that if some terrible emergency happened she would get in touch with me, she had that sense at any rate.

I became cold. It was as if my heart stopped pumping the warm blood round my body. My hands were permanently cold, and my feet; my body suddenly would tremble violently for no apparent reason, and I would have to lean against a wall, a table, or hold onto my chair in order to remain upright. I spoke to the doctor about this, but all he did was mumble incomprehensibly about my working too hard. I should take up fishing like my father-in-law, or golf; he himself was a golfing man and there was much good in the game. Yes, yes, yes. No doubt a few rounds of golf played regularly would do me all the good in the world. Meanwhile don't overdo the work. I didn't like to tell him that my heart was broken. It sounds absurd, but it was the truth.

For two years there was no sound from her and then one day I was walking down Angelsea Road towards St Mary's; it was a cold winter day, grey, the sky promising a lot of rain, the wind blowing pieces of paper and grit

in circular movements along the road. As I crossed the
road to get to the church a woman appeared from
behind the gate. She stood on the gravel, holding by the
hand a small child. She seemed to be waiting for me. I
took off my hat as I reached her.

'Dadda.'

The trembling started again, the icy shivering, quite
uncontrollable. I leant for a moment against the gate for
support. She stepped towards me and threw her arms
around me.

'Dadda.'

'Come.' It was all. I could say. 'Come.'

I pulled her across the gravel to the church door and
she pulled the child after her. We must have looked a
weird bunch. I pushed the door and we went into the
porch. We stared at each other for a long time and the
child stared at us.

'My dear girl.'

'You look so tired.' She touched my face gently.

I shook my head. 'I have trouble sleeping. But you . . .
you're grown-up. Yes. You're not . . . You're grown-up.
I wouldn't have recognised you.'

'Yes, you would.'

She stepped away from me and grasped the small
child's hand.

'Have you come home? For good?'

'I have come back to Ireland. For good, yes. Did she not tell you?'

'Who?'

'Mummy. I spoke to her on the phone the day before yesterday. She didn't sound best pleased to hear my voice.'

'Not a word. She never said . . .'

'I thought she might not, so I decided to come and find you for myself. By the way this is Sally.'

She pulled the child against her and held her tight.

'I wonder why she didn't . . .'

'Dadda, listen to me. This is Sally.'

I smiled at the little girl. She stared back.

'I told Mummy about her.'

'You mean . . .?'

'Oh for God's sake, Dadda. Use your bloody brains. This is my Sally. She's mine. I haven't borrowed her for the day.'

I was confused.

I stepped into the nave of the church and sat down in the back pew. The heating was off; we could only afford to take the chill off the air at weekends. Ruth and the child followed me, their feet making a loud clattering on the bare floor.

'She's your child.'

'Yes.'

'And you told your mother about her?'

'Yes.' Her voice was impatient.

'I see. I take it this means you aren't married.' There was a long silence. The child kicked with her foot at the corner of the pew.

'Don't do that, darling,' Ruth said. The child paid no heed. 'Of course I'm not married.'

'That would have upset your mother. May I ask who...? I mean to say ... yes, well may I ask...?'

She let go of the child and took a step back then swung her arm back and slapped me hard on the face. The child began to cry; she bent and picked her up and stood looking at me.

'What are you saying? What sort of a person do you think I am? You bastard. You fucking perverted bastard. How can you ask me such a question?'

She was screaming and the child was crying and the church caught the sounds and whirled them round and round. I heard the words over and over again.

My cheek was stinging.

I leant my head on the pew in front and tried to battle with the words, but they flew like evening bats round and round the church; the air was filled with the noise with the meaning, the terrible meaning, and there was the sound of my heart beating as if it were going to burst. When finally I had the strength to look up, she was gone, the child was gone; there only remained a small woollen glove on the floor. I stooped down and picked it up and put it in my pocket.

My child.

My cheek was still stinging: I put my hand up to it; it was feverishly hot.

My child.

I took the glove from my pocket and stared at it. It was pale, fluffy, blue wool. She might need it this cold day, I thought.

My child.

What had she called her?

Sally.

My child, Sally.

I put the glove back in my pocket.

There must be a terrible punishment for this. God or no God.

Unto the third or fourth generation.

My child.

I wondered at that moment should I kill myself, pollute the church. The sexton would find my body stretched across the altar, blood congealing on the tiled floor, or hanging perhaps in the vestry. I could just go away, disappear into the darkness, the glory of darkness and silence.

Push away such thoughts. Such rubbish thoughts.

Where would that get anyone?

Answer me that.

Following two such sins with another.

My child?

Yes.

I had never even thought of such a possibility.

Perhaps I am what she called me, a fucking perverted bastard.

It certainly didn't seem like that at the time. It doesn't seem like that now.

No.

I was cold. My hands, my feet, my whole body, apart from my stinging cheek, frozen.

I had to stand up. I had to go out of this church. I had to get warm. I had to be able to think once more.

I would never have comfort again.

I got up. I stood stooped like an old man, full of stiffness. I walked with the stiff steps of an old man, my hand groping out for support. Perhaps they will be waiting outside, my children, hidden in the bushes by the gate. Perhaps we could run away, the three of us, and reinvent ourselves, live blameless, happy lives in some other country, be tender and gentle with each other.

I pulled myself together and stood upright, I ordered my clothes and rubbed my face, then I opened the door and went out. No one was there, either on the gravel sweep or hiding in the bushes. Unconcerned cars drove past the gate and a woman pushed a large pram along the pavement. I stepped out into the daylight and closed the door behind me.

I did what I have always done when my mind is boiling, I walked. Down Simonscourt Road and across Merrion Road and straight on down to Sandymount and then as far as the sea. The tide was high and the wind blew ruffles of water that splashed against the wall and sent showers of drops over onto the pavement.

I wondered what Ruth had told her mother. I wondered had she told her everything there was to tell. Blown the whistle. I didn't think she would have done that.

I sat on a seat looking out over the sea wall towards Howth. Birds drifted on the wind. I would give Ruth money. I would make sure that she did not have that sort of problem. Everything would be all right. I would not see either her or the child.

I would work.

I would bring more and more people to the golden feet of God.

My sermons, my speeches, my essays would charge us to embrace each other, would shout the glories of ecumenism: Romans, Anglicans, Methodists, Presbyterians and Orthodox would all one day honour each other, one huge family, well knit, well ordered. Then, having consolidated our own love and trust, we would turn with our arms open towards the Jews, Muslims, Hindus, to everyone. The family of the human being would become one. Then would we turn our swords into ploughshares.

That would be my punishment.

I began to laugh. I sat on the seat with spray coming over the wall, shining as it fell around my feet.

My black secret would be locked away.

I laughed.

I threw back my head and laughed.

I was of course mad, but no one would ever know.

I took my handkerchief from my pocket and wiped my eyes. My cheek was still sore where she had hit me.

I never thought at that moment about how she would also be punished and her child: unto the third and fourth generation, that was what the Book said. Unto the third or fourth generation. I never gave a thought to any of that until Ruth, my beloved Ruth, killed herself and then I began to know the meaning of punishment.

Now you know what I have wished to tell you. Maybe it is the truth at last. Maybe I should not have written this letter. Maybe all these things would have been better left unsaid.

It was you who said 'I have you and you have me, for what it's worth.' Something along those lines. That was what put the thought into my head.

That was when I felt that truth ... what the hell is truth anyway? My whole life has been a great untruth and here I am at the end of it wanting to put things right. Except of course the truth may cause more pain than any of us need.

How do we know?

Or as you would probably say, how do we fucking know?

Inelegant but contemporary.

My hand and my head are weary; I hope you can read my shaky writing.

Now that this cat is out of its bag I do not know what I should call you so I will just say my dear Sally. My dear, dear Sally, if you were to come and hold my hand perhaps the warmth might creep from your fingers up my arm and into my old body that has been cold for so long.

When I got home I threw the bundle of papers onto the table in the sitting room and went into the kitchen. Everything was shining.

God bless Mrs Murdoch, long live Mrs Murdoch. May Mrs Murdoch live for ever. I love this order, I thought, even if I am alone. It saves me from total despair. The red light on the answering machine was flashing: message one, ring agent; message two, ring director; message three ring Charlie. I deleted all three. They would no doubt all ring again.

I switched on the television; war still ongoing.

I put on the kettle and made myself some toast: two large pieces, lots of butter and Marmite, black, black, black coffee. I settled myself on the sofa with a rug wrapped round my knees.

The war was the same as it had always been, clouds of black smoke still rose up behind the commentators, no signs yet of the promised weapons of mass destruction, people ugly in their sorrow and fear, mutilations, blood, dirty bandages. I switched off the set and lay staring up at the ceiling.

I must give up this stupid father nonsense, I thought; I am halfway through my life without a father, I can continue to the end.

Yes. Surely I can do that?

I will pull out all the Pegeen Mike stops and then forget the bloody woman. Never even go and see the play again.

Oh God, how I love toast and Marmite; that would be my last meal if I were about to be executed. The victim ate a hearty breakfast of toast and Marmite, she went to her death with that taste stinging the inside of her mouth.

Synge's own direction is: 'she pulls the shawl over her head and breaks out into wild lamentations.' Like those women in Iraq, like the Palestinian women we see whose husbands have been blown up by Jewish bombs; that is where I have to go. Lamentation is such a wonderful word. We don't use it any more and yet the world is more full of lamentation than ever before. I have grieved all my life over a father that I have never known. And, I grieve for Charlie.

Oh, yes.

My mind is seriously wandering.

I wonder why we feel we have to be loved best, all the time?

Is this why people believe in God?

Laughter.

It can't be such a notion.

Such an absurd notion.

I suppose it's where parents come in handy; they love their children better than they love anyone else.

I suppose they are looking at themselves, their dreams, their wild notions, then their cheeky, absurd children reject all that stuff and yet their parents go on loving them.

Was Moth like that?

I don't think so. Her self-hatred was so intense, it so filled her life that she had no room for anything else: no fun, no love, no friends, no bloody staying power. If you hadn't had me I wonder would you have done that thing earlier in your life?

That self snuffing.

Or maybe not at all.

How I hate this sort of musing. It carries you along like a sharply flowing river, to some unknown destination; you have to scramble out before it is too late, strike for the shore.

Yes.

That is what I must do.

Get the ground beneath my feet.

Get up from this sofa, go and do something, stupid

woman; make some more toast and Marmite, read a book, gaze at Pegeen Mike with energy, telephone those people who telephoned you, wash your hair. Do something.

Anything.

I might dance.

I threw the rug off my knees and got up.

Old-fashioned dancing.

I rustled through the CDs until I found a suitable disc.

They asked me how I knew, my true love was true
I of course replied, something here inside, cannot be deni . . . ied.
They said some day you'll find all who love are blind.
When your heart's on fire, you must realise
Smoke gets in your eyes.

Slow, quick, quick, slow.

Cool clipped voice singing the words.

So I chaffed them and I gaily laughed to think they could doubt my
love

Quick, quick, slow an. . .d a slow and languorous turn.

Yet today my love has flown away,
I am without my love.

Charlie was a good dancer.

Old and new variety.

I twirled towards the window and saw four faces gazing in on me, solemn, not giggling.

Now laughing friends deride tears I cannot hide
So I smile and say, when a lovely flame dies,
Smoke gets in your eyes,
Smoke gets in your eyes.

Turn and curtsy to the watchers.

They clap.

Bless their cotton socks.

I opened the door. 'Come in and dance,' I said to them.

They trooped in.

'We thought you'd never ask,' said Brendan.

'I just wanted a little dance on my own.'

'Tutt,' he said.

We danced, we swirled, booped, jumped, slid. We did a bit of hip-hop and jived and then we all had lemonade.

'That was good,' said Brendan. 'Thanks.'

'Yeah. Thanks.'

'Thanks.'

'Thanks.'

And they all left.

I felt better.

I re-ordered the furniture.

I got out a bottle of white wine from the fridge.

I got the old man's papers and sat down to read them.

* * *

When the gods wants to punish us they grant our requests.

Who was it said that?

I haven't got the foggiest idea.

I want to scream; but the noise of my scream would deafen the world.

This is not my fault.

I must keep saying that, for ever.

On and on.

Sally, you fool, you pathetic half-person, this is not your fault.

Someone Greek I bet said those words.

Yes.

I can't even cry.

The inside of my head is raw and dry. No tears, just this threatening scream.

I must not scream.

After all I have lived this long, I have survived I feel I should say, therefore I must continue.

Yes.

Down the long road.

Pathetic half-person.

Dark road.

Come, come. Is it any darker than it was half an hour ago?

Isn't it just convention makes this such a sin?

No.

The Greeks said it was a sin.

They knew.

They punished the perpetrators and the innocent victims. They were punished also. As he said, to the third and fourth generations.

Perhaps this is why I refused to have Charlie's children: somewhere inside myself I knew.

Naaah.

It is not my fault.

I can say that aloud and with conviction.

Not.

My.

Fault.

Such beautiful words.

But they only mean something if you believe them.

Oh Moth. Bloody, bloody Moth. How could you have done this to me?

Laughter.

Yes, laughter.

How could you have done it to yourself?

That's really what I meant to say.

How could you not for one moment have thought about your glorious future: career, lovers, marriage, the possibility of real children spreading around you, making you laugh.

What did you have, bloody Moth?

Depression and death.

Me. Pathetic half-person. You had me. Wanting to know, always the one thing you couldn't tell me.

Laughter.

I hear it all around me beating my head, inside and outside, wave upon wave of laughter.

Can you drown in laughter?

Perhaps he and I have done the only thing possible, act. You didn't have the ability to do that.

I can forget everything in other people's words. I can fill my brain with their song. Day after day, night after night. Thousands upon thousands of words.

Is that where the answers are?

In those words?

Maybe there are no answers.

Only questions.

Questions.

Questing.

He, of course, on the other hand, his whole life since then, since that day she left him in that horrible house in Ailesbury Road, since then, no, no, I do have to say that was not the moment when he started his life of lying. No. Oh how I feel pity for the poor brute.

His brittle carapace of sanctity now shattered.

If I were to blow the whistle on him, even now they could drag him into the courts, throw him into gaol, expose him to the world for what he is. What was it she called him?

Fucking perverted bastard.

A pathetic sham, would be more like.

How can I hate him?

How can you hate anyone so pathetic?

He is all I have left.

He is half of me.

More than half of me, if you look at it carefully.

I don't think I can love him either.

Or honour him.

No. I definitely cannot do that.

I am, of course, all that he has left also.

Think of that, girl.

Tomorrow, when I wake, or think I do, what shall I say of today?
That with Estragon my friend, at this place, until the fall of night,

I waited for Godot?
That Pozzo passed, with his carrier, and that he spoke to us?
Probably.
But in all that what truth will there be?

Laughter again.
    Always laughter.

    The air is full of our cries. But habit is a great deadener.

We have to go on.
    This half person has to go on.
    One day I'll play Vladimir, in spite of them all.
    Perhaps to spite them all.
    Do I have to call him Dadda now, as she did?
    Or shall we never mention this?
    Take it as read and then locked away.
    Sssh.
    Grandfather.
    It has been such a recent acquaintanceship.
    Grandfather, I think.
    Sssh.
    Grandfather.
    Why did you tell me?
    It's a piece of news I'd rather not have known.

If you had died without telling me I could have continued my grumbling and searching for ever.

Not happy, I will admit, but it had become a way of life for me.

Maybe I will become lost now.

I don't want to become lost.

No, I really don't.

Telephone.

My legs carried me to the telephone, then I crumbled into a chair.

'Hello.'

'Hi, Sal . . .'

'Charlie.'

Then the tears flooded out of me and I was not able to speak. I put the receiver on the table and covering my face with my hands I howled.

Words squawked from the set, words I couldn't hear.

'Sally . . . Sal . . . darling . . . hang on . . . I'll be there . . . Sal . . . be there. Now.'

I sat and waited and howled for what seemed like hours, but of course it wasn't. He knocked and rang simultaneously, and I think gave the bottom of the door a kick. I opened it and stood looking at him.

'Sally.' He stepped into the hall. 'My God, look at you. What the hell is the matter?' He put his arm gently round my shoulders and led me back into the sitting room. He pushed me down onto the sofa, tucking cushions around me and then the rug over my legs. He blew softly through his teeth as he arranged me, made me comfortable. 'I'm putting on the kettle. I'm not going away. You need coffee. I'm not going away Sal. Just coffee and then you can tell me what this is all about.'

He left the room and I could hear those comfortable sounds that indicate that someone is attending to things. He came back into the room with a basin of warm water and a cloth.

'The old face needs a bit of attention.'

'Thank you.'

I wiped my eyes.

He pulled the curtains.

The warm water was soothing; I patted it onto my face and neck. I closed my eyes and saw the coloured stars dancing. I heard his feet passing to and fro. He dried my face gently; he carried away the basin. He blew softly through his teeth as he moved.

I kept my eyes shut. I needed to do that. I needed that quietude.

The coloured stars whirled.

Blotting out.

The comfortable sounds of his footfalls. Cupboards

opened and shut. The clink and chinks of preparation and the coloured stars danced.

'There you are, doll.'

I opened my eyes and he put a mug of coffee on the table beside me. 'Like some scrambled eggs? I could do some in a minute.'

'No. Thanks, Charlie. This is great. Thank you for coming.'

He sat down on the sofa beside me. 'If you'd heard yourself on the phone, you'd have been here like greased lightning. Have a slurp of coffee and then tell me what's up.'

He must have put a slug of brandy in the coffee; the circulation of warmth not only hit me in the core of my stomach but also in my hands and feet; my blood which had seemed congealed began to move again.

He sat crouched beside me, his eyes searching my face. 'OK. Shoot.'

'I'd rather you read it yourself.'

'Read what?'

'His piece. Grandfather's piece. It's there on the table. I'd rather . . .'

He got up and went over to the table. He picked up the papers and tapped them together neatly.

'Where . . .?' He waved the bundle at me.

'Anywhere you like. I'm just going to lie here with my

eyes shut. This coffee is the most wonderful thing that has ever happened to me.'

'Ever?'

'Well, not quite ever, but certainly in the last two hours.'

He nodded and left the room; I heard him going upstairs. I heard nothing else; the house was quite silent. I imagined him sitting in the room that had been his work room, turning the pages slowly, letting each one drop to the floor after he had finished it. I listened for the sound of his quiet breathing, the little whistling noises that he made when he was concentrating, the whisper of the pages as they floated from his hand to the floor. I heard nothing. I slept, no dreams, just deep sleep.

When I woke he was sitting on the other end of the sofa, his hands loosely clasped on his knees, his eyes shut.

'Charlie,' I whispered.

His eyes opened at once; he had not been sleeping, just waiting for me to wake.

He stretched out a hand to me. I took it and he pulled me slowly towards him until I rested against him, my head on his shoulder.

'Darling Sally.' Those were his first words. 'Do you believe it?'

I nodded.

'Why wouldn't I?'

'Indeed.'

He held me very tight, almost as if he thought that at any moment I might fall apart.

'Look,' he spoke into my hair. 'There's just one thing I'd like to say, before you say anything. I love you, OK? I've loved you for an age and I always will. I know I'm a bit of a skirt-chaser but I love you. I want to come back and live with you. I don't give a damn about babies and all that shit. I just love you. I want to be around you. I'll even forgive you for throwing coffee over my new shoes. I want to come back, I've been so lonely without you. I don't make any rash promises about never chasing skirts again, but you are my one enduring love, my sister, my mother, my lover, my friend.'

I heard every word he said through the top of my head.

'I'm only half a person.'

'So? What does that matter? Who cares? I don't.'

'I do.'

'Nothing has changed. You're still you, except now you know it all. For God's sake, Sal, it's not as if he was a mass murderer, Saddam Hussein, Slobodan Milosevic, Stalin. Then you might worry about blood lines, about guilt. He's just a pathetic old Church of Ireland bishop who has told lies all his life because he didn't have the guts to say boo to his father and mother. You're not pathetic. You're a star, a bright shining star. You are what he didn't have the courage to be. I know he destroyed your mother, but she was filled with all his weaknesses; you're not like her. She was a decent enough woman, but she should have told someone, not let herself be eaten up the way she was. She certainly should have told you. You could have held her hand and given her strength. That's what people need. Strength. Of course you care. I care too. I care because I want you to be happy, be free, to love living, to trust people, I'm sounding like a bloody counsellor, amn't I?' He shook me by the shoulders. 'Amn't I? Am I not, Sal?'

'Yes.'

He kissed the top of my head.

'Are you laughing at me?'

'No.'

'Do you love me?'

'Yes.'

'Do you know what the time is?'

I laughed. 'I haven't the foggiest idea.'

'Four thirty a.m.' He whispered the words.

'Charlie! I don't believe it.'

'True.'

I looked at my watch. It was true.

'Would you like to know what I think we should do?'

'You must go. Now. Go, go, go.' I waved my arms at him. 'And I must go, go, go to bed. Tomorrow . . . today . . .'

He took my hands in his. 'Listen to me. Shut up, Sal. You are going to bed and to sleep and I am going to stay here.'

'What about Marianna?'

'Bugger Marianna.'

'That's not very kind.'

'Enough, enough. Don't you start telling me I'm a bastard. Just go to bed, sleep and when you wake up I will be here and . . .'

'And what?'

'Let's see then. Go on, now. Bed.'

I was too tired to argue with him.

* * *

Voices. The chuckle of laughter. The seductive smell of bacon frying. A burst of coughing from Mrs Murdoch.

I remembered.

I pulled open my eyes and stared at the window; the curtains stirred in the wind, rain scattered. There was another burst of laughter from downstairs.

What the hell did all this matter?

I will go and see him and tell him that.

Yes.

I pushed back the warm bedclothes and got out of bed.

It was a horrible day; my garden looked like the First World War had happened there.

I will go and tell him that I love him in spite of everything, in spite of what he did to my mother.

'Sal.'

I put on my dressing gown and ran a comb through my hair.

'We can hear you plonking round. Breakfast is ready. You need breakfast. Come on down.'

The pair of them were sitting at the kitchen table when I arrived.

'Didn't I tell you he'd be back?' said Mrs Murdoch through a mouthful of food.

'By the skin of his teeth,' I said.

'Back is back,' said Charlie. 'And I notice I left my old school photographs in the hall. That should have said something to you. You don't honestly think I would have gone permanently without them.'

He shovelled food onto my plate. Bacon, egg, sausages, fried bread.

'Anyway how could I live without Mrs M. in my life? Answer me that.'

I sat down and began to eat. He turned to Mrs Murdoch. 'She doesn't speak.'

'Could you be serious for a minute or two? Haven't you her heart broken and you can't mend that in a jiffy. I must get on with my little job.' She heaved herself up from the table and left the room.

'I love that woman. I love her nearly as much as I love you. I don't know anyone else who can cook bacon as she does. Not even my mother.' He took a piece of bacon from my plate and scrunched it in his mouth.

'Oh Charlie, your mother . . .'

'She'll be so pleased, she's been at me and at me and she hated Marianna. She couldn't abide her.'

'Look, about your mother . . .'

He leant forwards me and put his hand on mine.

'What my mother doesn't know won't hurt her. Look, we don't have to tell anyone, or we can tell the world. You can go to the doctor, you can go to the police. It doesn't matter. It's up to you. Only you and me of course. I'm with you whatever you decide.'

I poured myself a cup of tea.

'I slept like a log,' I said to him. 'I didn't think I'd ever sleep again, but there you are. We are such odd things, we, bloody people. Aren't we? I found out something I'd always wanted to know. Something so important to me there had been times I thought I couldn't go on without knowing. And now . . . and now that I know I can put up with it. This halfness. I think I can. Cope. Yes. I do think I can cope. What happened during sleep? Some sort of commonsensical soothing? Massaging of the brain cells? Have a cup of tea?'

He shook his head.

'Why aren't you at work anyway?

'Because I'm here with you. You need me, just for a while, and I'm here. Make the best of it.'

'Being confused upsets me.'

'I think it upsets everyone.'

'I have to go and see him.'

'Yes. That's clear. That's not confused in any way. Do you want me to come with you?'

'Would you? I might want you to sit in the car. Be invisible. I'm not sure. Would you mind that?'

'I'll do whatever you want me to do.'

'Poor old Moth.'

'Yes.'

'Do you think she'd mind?'

He thought for a long time.

I drank my tea and watched his face.

'I think she'd be relieved. It's a terrible burden to carry on your own. It's such a black secret. I feel she would have been looking over her shoulder all the time, waiting for retribution of some sort. They were the sinners, not you. You are the totally innocent victim.'

'Poor old Moth.'

'Yeah, well you can say that for ever if you want to.' He threw his head back and began to sing. 'For evah and evah, evah and evah . . .'

I laughed. 'You're such a twit.'

'Thank you. I do like to be appreciated.'

'She was so unlike a sinner.'

'You just want him to shoulder all the blame?'

'I suppose so. But . . .'

'But what?'

'Let's leave it. I'll go and get dressed and we'll go to Howth.'

The telephone rang. Charlie stretched out a hand and picked up the receiver. 'Hi. Oh hi. How are you? What do you mean what am I doing here? No. She's changed her mind. Yes. She's here. Yes. I expect she'll speak to you. Will you speak to David?'

I held out my hand for the phone.

'Yep. Here she is. See you sometime.' He put the receiver into my hand and wiggled his eyebrows.

'Hello, David.'

'Hello, beautiful lady. He's back.'

'Yes.'

'Is that good or bad?'

'As he's standing here beside me, listening, I have to say, good. I'm sorry I didn't ring you back yesterday, but I was in very late.'

'When are you off?'

'We start rehearsing on Monday and go on Friday.'

'I spoke to Miramax about you playing Clara. They want to see you in New York. I think this will happen, doll. Will you behave?'

'I always behave.'

'You know what I mean.'

'Of course I'll behave.'

'I'll tell them that's all right then. I'll fly out and we can see them together.'

'There's no need for that.'

'I want to see *Playboy* anyway.'

'Suit yourself. Look, I must go. Can you ring me another time?'

'I will be coming to New York. Get that into your head, Sally. I'll be in touch. 'Bye, my darling. Kiss, kiss and one for Charlie too.'

'Kiss,' I said. I put the receiver down.

'Life goes on.'

* * *

We drove in his comfortable BMW to Howth. The rain was relentless, the clouds black and low, bursting with water, the wipers worked overtime. From Grandfather's house you could barely see the city.

There was a light on over the hall door as if they were expecting us.

I sat in the car, my hands clenched tightly together. 'I'm frightened.'

Charlie put his arm round my shoulders and kissed my cheek. 'It's all right, love. Don't worry. Go now. The longer you hesitate the worse it will get. Go, go.' He gave me a gentle push. I opened the door. Rain poured in. 'Quick or we'll all drown.'

I got out and ran to the door. Mrs Carruthers must have been looking out of the window because the door was open by the time I reached it.

She stood in the hall. She looked pale and tired.

'He said you'd come. Is that your husband in the car? Would he like in out of the rain? There's a fire in the drawing room. He could have a cup of coffee.'

'Thank you.'

As I put my head out of the door to call to Charlie there was a huge crash of thunder and almost immediately a flash of lightning ripped across the sky. Before I had time to open my mouth he was out of the car and into the house.

'Oh my God!'

Mrs Carruthers closed the door.

'Mrs Carruthers, this is my husband, Charlie. He hates thunder.'

'No, no, no. How do you do. It's the lightning. I have to

admit to total terror when that happens. The rolling and rumbling of thunder I don't mind at all. It's the other stuff. Please forgive me.'

'I don't like it very much myself, sir.' There was a glimmer of a smile on her face. 'Perhaps you might prefer to sit in the kitchen with me. There is a fire in the . . .'

'How kind you are.'

'If you'll just wait a moment, sir, I must bring Sally to his Lordship's room. He's in bed. I'm afraid he's not at all well. We had a very bad night.'

Charlie patted my shoulder.

'I'll be all right, darling. Mrs Carruthers will take good care of me.'

There was a log fire crackling in the grate, casting jumping shadows on the ceiling. The curtains were tightly pulled, the air was second-hand. The lamp on the table by his bed shone on his pale face and his hair.

Under his eyes were huge black hollows; no one had shaved him that morning. He was propped up by several pillows and it looked as if the covers were too heavy for his body to bear. I tiptoed to the bed, not sure if he was awake or asleep. I stood and stared down at him. He looked so tired, almost too tired to be alive. Is this what letting loose your secrets does to you? His hands lay unmoving outside the covers. I put out one of my hands and gently touched one of his. It was cold, but stirred slightly as I touched him.

'Sit. Don't stand. Sit. She put a chair there for you to sit on.' His voice was quite strong.

I sat. His eyes were now open and looking at me. He grasped my hand and clung on to it.

'I knew you would come.'

'Grandfather . . .'

'Heh heh heh.' He laughed for a moment and then was silent.

'You can laugh.' That sounded bitter. 'I didn't mean to be rude. I'm sorry. What should I call you?'

He was silent.

'If you don't know, how the hell can I?'

His fingers scrabbled at mine.

'I have wanted to die for so long,' he said.

I put my other hand over his; there was nothing of him, a few old bones held together by a tatter of skin. I had been fooled by his air of dignity, the way he had held his body upright. All his life he had fooled us, everyone except Moth, poor old Moth.

A wave of fury rose up inside me and I thought how easy it would be to kill him, just put one of those pillows over his face. It would only take a few moments and very little pressure.

'You see.' He pulled his hand away from mine. 'I may not

believe in God, but I do believe in good and evil. My dear Sally, do not forget that evil begets evil and again and again.'

I wondered how he knew what I had been thinking.

'I've read your letter. Is it fact or fiction?'

'What do you want me to say?'

'The truth.'

'It is fact, of course. So? Do you hate me?'

'What do you want me to say?'

'The truth.'

'I want to hate you, for what you did to my mother. For what you did to yourself and me. Of course there's me. A freak of some sort. That's what I am. You've handed me a secret I don't want. No one would ever want that sort of secret. No one. I want to hate you for that and your sanctimonious religiosity. How dare you become a bishop. How dare you have that honoured position—'

'My dear girl,' he interrupted me. 'Far worse men than I, worse sinners than I, have become bishops. Don't let's bring the Church into this. Murderers, embezzlers, thieves, womanisers, scoundrels of many hues. The history of the Church is filled with men who you would consider unworthy. Men you would cross the road to avoid. Devils as well as angels. Just remember that when you start pointing the finger.'

He was exhausted by the speech and his eyes closed.

I got up and went over to the window. I pulled back the heavy curtains, the clouds wrapped round us; I could barely see the hedge at the bottom of the garden. The thunder seemed to have passed but the rain steadily beat on the windows; the drops exploded as they hit the glass and then leapt, raced down to the already saturated ground.

'I don't hate you.'

'Pull those curtains. I cannot bear looking at that rain.'

I pulled them tight, not leaving the smallest crack.

'Come here. Fix my pillows for me. I wish to sit up.'

I went back to the bed and pulled him up and tucked pillows in behind him.

'Thank you. Thank you. That will do. That will be all right.'

He pulled at his hair with a hand.

'I do so dislike being unwell. I do so dislike not being in charge. Moaning and mumbling. Where is that woman?'

'What woman?'

'Mrs Carruthers. She was to bring you coffee.'

'She'll come. Don't fret. She's giving my husband coffee. Then she'll come.'

'Your husband?'

'Yes. He's afraid of thunder. So he's quaking in the kitchen.'

'I thought he'd gone. Left you.'

'He came back. I needed him. He's read your ... he knows.'

'He knows?'

'Yes.'

'Is that wise.'

I laughed.

'Of course it's wise. I don't know what you expected me to do, Grandfather. I told Charlie. That's all I'm going to do.'

'Ring the bell for the woman.'

'She'll come in her own time.'

I sat down by the bed again, pulling the chair close beside him. I reached out and took his hand. I bent and kissed it. His fingers fluttered as my lips pressed against them.

'What did you do that for?'

'Didn't you hear what I said?'

'When? What?'

'I don't hate you. I can't. I keep saying you must hate him to myself, but it doesn't work. I quite like you. You're all I have anyway. I've had this dream all these years that I'd find my father one day and with him a whole new history. Now I'm just stuck with you ... and you want to die and then ...'

'And then?'

'It will just be me and Charlie. And, of course Shakespeare and Chekhov and Beckett and all those other people whose words will fill my head. I'll act for you, every part I do I'll ask myself what would he have thought of this. Was that good enough for him? Yep. That's what I'll do. And you can sit with your other rascal bishops wherever that will be and look down at me and say to them she's mine. Of her I am very proud. Will you do that?'

'You don't hate me?'

I shook my head.

The door opened and Mrs Carruthers came in with a tray; a silver coffee pot gleamed and cups and saucers clinked together as she walked across the room.

'Leave it,' he said. 'There. Leave it there on the table. She can pour out.'

Without a word Mrs Carruthers put the tray on the table and left the room.

'Help yourself,' he said when the door was closed.

'In a while.'

We sat in silence; the fire spat and crackled and the rain battered on the window. I held his hand. His eyes were open and he stared straight ahead. My fingers gently stroked his wrist.

'She was so beautiful,' he said at last. 'I meant her no harm. I promise you that.'

'I know, Grandfather.'

'Will you ever forgive me?'

'I have. I do. I always will.'

I leant over and kissed his cheek.

'Will you do something for me?'

'Of course.'

He put his hand and covered the spot where I had kissed him.

'It mustn't disappear.'

'It won't and anyway there's more where that came from.'

'My dear child.'

'What do you want me to do?'

'Read for me.'

'Of course. What would you like me to read?'

'There on the table. The beginning of St John. If you please.'

I picked up the Bible.

He held my hand tight in his so I had to fumble through the tissue pages to find St John. I looked at him. He nodded and smiled at me.

'That's a good girl. My girl.'

I began to read.

'In the beginning was the Word, and the Word was with God and the Word was God.

The same was in the beginning with God.

All things were made by him; and without him was not any thing made that was made.

In him was life; and the life was the light of men.

And the light shineth in darkness and the darkness comprehended it not.

There was a man, sent from God, whose name was John.

The same came for a witness, to bear witness of the light, that all men through him might believe.

He was not that light, but was sent to bear witness of that light.

That was the true light, which lighteth every man that cometh into the world.

He was in the world and the world was made by him and the world knew him not.

He came unto his own and his own received him not.

But as many as received him, to them gave he power to become the sons of God, even to them that believe on his name;

Which were born, not of blood, nor of the will of the flesh, nor of the will of man, but of God.

And the Word was made flesh and dwelt among us (and we beheld his glory, the glory as of the only begotten of the Father) full of grace and truth.'

He had spoken the words with me to begin with, his voice strong and rotund.

'*And the light shineth in darkness and the darkness comprehended it not.'*

We both spoke those words together. Then he became

silent, listening with care to the marvellous words.

He fell asleep, leaning sideways in the bed. He looked secure and comfortable.

Gently I pulled my hand from his and went to pour myself some coffee. I walked on tiptoe across the room thinking about poetry and grace and truth.

There was no sound in the room, not even from the fire which had crumbled down into itself. I looked towards the bed and the light still shone on his face and hair. He was so still, his head bent down into the pillows, his hands still, outside the covers. I put down my coffee and went over to the bed. He just looked as if he were asleep. I took his hand and kissed it again and then sat by him in the chair, holding his hand gently in mine, and the firelight flickered around us both and the coffee became cold.